To Phoebe
with love Gramma

ADAM LONGDEN

Adam Longden © Copyright 2019

The moral right of Adam Longden to be identified as the author of this work has been asserted in accordance with the Copyright, Designs and patents Act 1988.

No part of this publication may be reproduced, stored in a retrieval system, or transmitted in any form or by any means without the prior permission in writing of the publisher. Nor be otherwise circulated in any form of binding or cover other than that in which it is published and without a similar condition including this condition being imposed on the subsequent purchaser.

This book is a work of fiction. The characters and incidents are either fictitious or are used fictitiously. Any resemblance to any real person or incident is entirely coincidental and not intended by the author.

All rights reserved.

This book is dedicated to all creatures, great and small...

CHAPTER 1

Text: *Have you seen my charger?* (grumpy face emoji). Mr Lewis waits, cup of coffee in hand, praying his phone will hold out. Typical: glued to Facebook twenty-four seven, but she never seems to notice texts or missed calls.

His phone vibrates on the desk. Hmm, he thinks, feeling a little harsh.

Text reply from Mrs Lewis: *Try in Lottie's Room. She was on the tablet x.*

Two things. First, the kiss thing: it irks him. A kiss used to mean something, like at the end of a love letter at school; it would make your heart pound. Or a Christmas card to the family from your nanna – one for each of the family members, three in their case. This is also acceptable. But now a kiss is at the end of every text. He even has the odd male friend who does it to him. This is definitely *not* acceptable. Secondly, the charger in Lottie's room. When did a tablet become a six-year-old's toy? What happened to crayons, snakes and ladders, tiddlywinks?

Deep breath.

Text reply: *Thanks* (no kiss).

Mr Lewis makes his way upstairs, petting the family cat on the way; his sole company on Monday mornings. It responds with a throaty, whistling rev, as if he's pushed a button on it – soft as grease, that thing. He doesn't mind it being him and the cat; he kind of looks forward to Mondays now. Whilst every other mug is up at the crack of dawn, beginning their commute or trying to beat the traffic before the school run, he is having a long shower, watching the morning news and having a leisurely breakfast.

There is a flipside. It means he has to work on Saturdays till one. He is an estate agent, a senior partner. Times are tough. Saturdays have become prime viewing time. And why pay someone else when you can do it yourself – more competently? It maddens him when they speak of these 'year on year' house price increases, or supposed 'buoyancy of the market' – not in his neck of the woods. London, maybe – it distorts the figures – and other pockets across the UK, but not round here. Every sale is like gold dust. They'd taken on a large mortgage when times were good; now they are paying for it. Things are tight. Too tight.

It had annoyed him at first, working Saturdays when you had underlings, but what would he be doing anyway? The weekly trip to the supermarket? No thanks. Mondays now mean catching up on emails, chasing up weekend viewings, planning the week ahead. He likes the peace and quiet, having the house to himself – a rare occurrence these days.

Eva: A grown-up fairy tale

His daughter's room is the usual mess – unmade bed, toys strewn about, chest of drawers open, clothes spilling from it, books everywhere – the weekend's hangover. At least she still reads from books, bless her; he knows some families who have taught their kids to read on damn tablets. He casts his eyes about, searching for the charger. No joy. He inspects the various plug sockets in the room. There it is, between the chest of drawers and the bed, still plugged in *and* switched on, tangled up around a book and a doll with outstretched arms. He unplugs the charger, extracting it from the doll, and places the book on the side. The doll he chucks onto the bed.

He turns to leave, coiling the charger around his hand. Then a movement on the bed catches his eye. His immediate thought is that the cat has brought in one of its presents, and this one has got away; it wouldn't be the first time. Fearing the worst, he scans the bed. To his astonishment, the dark-haired doll is sitting upright in its little outfit, rubbing its eyes. It looks like an early imitation Sindy or Barbie-type doll. Whatever it is, it's turning towards him and smiling. It has teeth; a choir of beautiful white teeth with a striking gap in them.

Mr Lewis recoils in horror. A strange sound escapes his throat. He is a pragmatic man, dogmatic, a realist; he doesn't believe in ghosts, God or Jesus. H. Christ himself – and he certainly doesn't believe in moving dolls! *What the hell?!* The doll stretches its arms out and shakes its wrists. 'Oh thank you, Mr Lewis, thank you! I knew you wouldn't let me down! I've been waiting for so long. I just needed to be touched by a man, a real man, and you *are* a real man, Mr Lewis. You are, you are, you are!' The doll calmly pulls itself across the covers, its movements all too human, to sit on the edge of the bed, its tiny legs dangling over the side.

'How ... how do you know my name?' says Mr Lewis, his face drained of colour; he is barely able to breathe.

'I can hear. I figured out the combination for that ages ago, but I've been trapped. I just needed you to touch me. I've been in this family for years, Mr Lewis. I've even been on holiday with you – Cornwall, remember?' The doll puts her hand over her mouth and giggles, as if remembering something amusing.

'Wait, what combination?'

'The numbers to unlock it. The same with sight; it's all about the numbers – they're like ingredients in a recipe. You just have to get the right ones in the right order. It's been so frustrating. I could see but I couldn't move my eyes – or anything for that matter...' Her voice has a melodious, charm-like quality to it – the tinkling of a babbling brook, the pealing of wedding bells on a May day. I'm conversing with a doll, Mr Lewis thinks. Have I gone mad? 'That is until now, thanks to you, my knight in shining armour!'

The doll hops off the bed, lands in a squat and does a cartwheel of glee across the floor. There is nothing jerky or puppet-like about her movements; they are full of grace. She is human; a miniature human. She skips over to Mr Lewis's trouser leg and begins to hug it.

Mr Lewis snaps out of the spell he's under and freaks out. 'Aaaggh! Get away from me!' He kicks his leg out, trying to shake the doll off, as if he's got a tarantula crawling up his trousers. The doll loses its grip and goes skidding across the carpet, letting out a squeal. Mr Lewis makes a run for it, dashing to the door and slamming it behind him. He stands with his back against it, breathing hard.

From the bedroom he hears the soft patter of movement, like the sound of the cat walking across the floor. Then he feels the thump of tiny fists on the door. 'Mr Lewis, come back. I didn't mean to scare you! Come back, my sweet prince!'

CHAPTER 2

Mr Lewis runs down the stairs, switches the computer off, grabs his keys and bolts for the front door. He can still hear that voice calling him, and maybe some sobs too. Or is everything in his head? Oh Christ, he thinks: I need to get out of here. The cat watches him leave, mildly curious at all the commotion. The front door slams. The cat goes back to washing its leg.

It's a short car journey into Uppingham, where Mr Lewis works. Sometimes he walks. Not today. On the way thoughts are racing through his brain. He knows he's been under a lot of pressure lately, financial pressure. I'm OK, aren't I? he thinks.

Neither of his agents are at their desks when he enters the office unannounced. What would that look like to potential buyers? A phone is ringing. This doesn't improve his state of mind. He can feel one of his migraines coming on. He picks up the phone, his hand shaking. 'Hello. Lewis-Allen Estate Agents.' At least it's some semblance of normality – something real. His two members of staff, Owen and Chantelle, scuttle in shamefaced at the sound of his voice. 'OK, madam, I'll just pass you over to my colleague who's been dealing with it.' False smile. He puts his hand over the mouthpiece. 'Mrs Peters, 104 The Willows. Deal with it!'

They swap places. The young man stinks like an ashtray. At least they haven't been shagging, then – unless it was a post-coital cigarette. 'Mrs Peters! Owen here. Good to hear from you.'

Mr Lewis gives Chantelle a look. 'I was just out the back making a coffee, Mr Lewis. Would you like one? We weren't expecting you in.'

'No, I can see that – and yes, strong, black, two sugars.' He'd never been a daytime drinker – it sends him to sleep – but right now he could do with something a little stronger. 'And two Paracetamol!'

Mr Lewis plugs in his phone and goes through the motions of work, trying to behave normally. He switches on the desk computer and opens up emails – exactly what he should be doing at home. He's looking at the screen but not seeing. He can't shake what's just happened from his mind. He can still hear that voice, still see that smile, the gap in those teeth.

Coffee is brought to him. He slurps from the mug, his hands still shaking. The liquid scalds his tongue. I've got to ring Dianne and tell her, he thinks, I must. Not here, though. On the mobile then, out the back. But tell her what? One of Lottie's dolls has come alive and spoken to me? She'd think I'd gone stark raving mad. His father had gone dotty early; she'd think he'd gone the same way. That or the pressure he'd been under. What if she divorced him? What if he couldn't see Lottie? What if he *had* imagined it? Was that worse? Calm down, calm down.

He decides not to tell her just yet. Let her find out for herself. That way he's covered both ways. He manages to send a few emails; he certainly can't speak to anyone on the phone just yet. The morning goes on. There are a couple of viewings coming up, and he decides to do them himself. Better to keep busy.

By lunchtime, Mr Lewis's work is pretty much done for the day. It was a quiet morning; nothing much going on. The phones still need answering, but *they* can do that. Normally he would go home for lunch on a day like this – call it a day, chill out for a bit, then go with his wife to pick his daughter up from school. But he can't go home yet – Dianne won't be back till two. He decides to go to the local brasserie in the square for some lunch instead; he could do with that drink.

Two dragged-out Peronis, a half-eaten BLT and a distracted look through the newspaper later, Mr Lewis heads back home. He pops a mint into his mouth before setting off: he shouldn't really be driving, but he's got bigger worries on his mind. It's gone two o'clock now. He keeps glancing at his phone on the passenger seat, expecting it to light up, to come alive and whirl round, vibrating – a panicked call from his wife. It doesn't.

He reaches their road, feeling anxious. Dianne should be home. Yes, there's her car. Good. A wave of relief washes over him. He can't believe it's come to this; he's afraid to be alone in his own home for fear of a doll, a toy – a child's plaything. He casts a nervous glance up at his daughter's bedroom window as he gets out of the car. Turning the key in the front door, he has no idea what to expect. Chaos? Silence?

It's the latter. He hangs his keys up on the hook at the bottom of the stairs, looking up to the landing, listening for sounds, eyes oscillating. Nothing. 'Hi. You're back early!' Mrs Lewis calls. It startles him. She's in the kitchen.

'Hi. Yes, quiet day – unfortunately. I popped in for a bit. Few viewings and that.' The rattling of pots can be heard.

'Do you want a cup of tea?'

'Er, yes please.'

His wife is at the sink. She looks up and smiles. Mr Lewis's first thought is to ask her if she's been upstairs yet, or into Lottie's room. But why would he be asking? 'How was your day?' he says instead, pushing down the button on the kettle.

'It's just boiled, actually,' she says. 'Oh, you know; the usual lunchtime rush – screaming kids with no manners...' She laughs. Mr Lewis fetches two mugs from a cupboard, leaning back to avoid the aggressive steam from the reboiled kettle. He places teabags in the mugs.

'I'll walk up with you in a bit to get Lottie,' he says, pouring in water.

'Oh, she's going straight to Sarah's today, remember?'

'What?' He misses the second mug entirely. 'Shit!' He leans across her to grab a sponge.

'Have you been drinking?'

'No. Why?' His wife gives his back a long look as he mops up the spillage.

'I told you this morning. You were watching the sports news if I remember, which would figure.' Great, he thinks. This is only going to prolong the agony. Finishing making the tea, he goes to the lounge with his. He decides to take matters into his own hands; to get it over and done with.

'I'm just going to get changed,' he says.

He makes his way upstairs, treading carefully, expecting the thing to wake up and start hollering. What excuse can he give for going into Lottie's room? Washing: he wasn't opposed to collecting the dirty laundry now and again. Reaching the landing, he pauses to listen. Nothing. He heads to Lottie's door and is about to turn the handle when something stops him. What if it starts calling him 'Mr Lewis' again, as if it knows him? Calling him 'my sweet prince' in that flirtatious sing-song voice? This would imply he's already acquainted with the thing. Jesus, pull yourself together, man. Listen to yourself, sneaking around, lying to your wife; you're not having an affair, for Christ's sake! What *is* this strange hold the doll has over him?

He quickly pushes open the door and walks in. The doll is nowhere to be seen. Where is it? Don't tell me it's got out somehow – that it's somewhere loose in the house? He scans the bed, the floor. He looks behind the door and starts in fright. There it is, thank God. Stationary, sitting with its arms outstretched – just a doll. He lets out a sigh of relief, then gives it a gentle nudge with his foot and steps back squeamishly, as he does with some of the cat's presents – a poor little bird or mouse – checking that they're dead before disposing of them. The doll doesn't move.

Mr Lewis gathers up some dirty clothes, satisfied for now, and leaves the room. He'll just put the whole thing down to an episode, an interlude, and move on, pretending it never happened.

****

'Daddy, can you come and give Lottie a kiss goodnight, please?'

'*Come on, Daddy!*' his daughter calls. Mr Lewis puts his bottle of beer down – his second of the evening – and gets up off the sofa. He never usually drinks on a Monday night; they try to have at least a couple of nights off during the week – and one is always a Monday. He still isn't quite feeling himself, though. There's no doubt about it; today's incident has unsettled him. Mrs Lewis has noticed it too. Her husband seems distracted, brooding.

'All ready for bed then?' he says, entering Lottie's bedroom.

'Yep. We've read *The Very Hungry Caterpillar*, haven't we, Mummy?'

'Well, *you* have darling. She's getting good.' Mrs Lewis strokes Lottie's hair. 'Nan-night then, sweetheart.' She gives her daughter a kiss and gets up from the bed. 'Daddy will tuck you in.'

'Nan-night, Mummy.' Mrs Lewis leaves the room.

'Nan-night then, sweetheart. Have you been to the loo?' Mr Lewis says, tucking Lottie in and kissing her.

'Yes.'

'Have you brushed your teeth?' Lottie nods, smiling. '*Mummy, has this little madam brushed her teeth?*'

'*Well, she says she has!*'

'Are you sure?' he says, tickling her. She giggles. 'Here, let me smell.' He leans in.

'You smell of beer, Daddy.'

'Never mind me. Breathe out.' No smell of mint. 'Go on,' he says. 'Go and brush your teeth.' Lottie stomps out of the room, groaning. Mr Lewis sighs. He *was* watching Monday Night Football.

He sits and waits. From along the landing he can hear the tinkling of the toilet bowl. Huh, so much for going to the loo. And no sound of teeth being brushed yet. Alone in the room, his thoughts turn to the doll. It still makes him uneasy. He gets up, searching for it. It is still where he left it, behind the door. Can't be one of her favourites then. I wonder if she'd miss it if I chucked it out? He goes over to pick the doll up and sits back down on the bed with it: big brown eyes with long lashes staring straight at him, raven hair, poppy red Cupid's bow lips. He gives its hair an experimental tug. Nothing. He peeps down the top of its khaki jacket – pale peach skin, hard plastic boobs. He laughs to himself, feeling foolish. What am I doing?

'What are you doing with Eva, Daddy?' Lottie startles him.

'Nothing. She was on the floor, that's all,' he says, putting the doll on the bed. 'Have you brushed your teeth?' Lottie blasts an icy-mint dragon's breath into his face before clambering into bed. He tucks her in. 'How do you know her name's Eva?'

''Cause I called her that, silly Daddy!'

'Oh, of course. Silly Daddy. Goodnight, angel. Sweet dreams.' Mr Lewis turns off the light and closes the door.

'Leave the door open just a bit!' Lottie calls.

'I will, don't worry.' He leaves the door ajar, then lingers on the landing for a moment. There's something about knowing the doll's name that concerns him. Don't they say not to learn the names of animals that you're going to put down? That it just makes it harder?

CHAPTER 3

Mr Lewis deliberates all week over what to do about the doll. He can't get it out of his mind. He wants to get rid of it. The doll represents something that doesn't fit into his way of thinking. He starts asking his daughter covert, roundabout questions to discern how attached to it she is. Questions about her five favourite toys or whether she prefers cuddly toys or dolls.

He spends so much time thinking about the doll that he begins to scare himself. Does he want it to come alive again or something? If only to prove one way or the other whether it happened or not? Now that the dust has settled, and now there seems no risk of it happening again, he can't help but feel a slight twinge of disappointment. The incident was the most exciting thing that had happened to him for some time – like a theme-park ride that scares you witless, but as soon as it's over you kind of want to do it again.

By the end of the weekend he hasn't seen Lottie play

with the doll once. And it certainly hasn't come back to life. He's even stared into its eyes a few times and waved his hand in front of its face. This decides it for him. Come tomorrow morning, the doll is going.

****

Monday morning, and Mr Lewis waves his wife and daughter off to work and school as normal. He's smiling, but there's a knot of trepidation in his stomach. He's been waiting for this moment all weekend. He has it all planned out. Tomorrow is recycling day, and so the grey bin goes out. He's going to stick the doll in there, bury it deep, then wheel the bin down the alleyway at the side of the house.

Closing the front door, he goes straight upstairs. He enters Lottie's room and looks for the doll. It would be typical if he couldn't find it. But no, there it is, protruding from the gap at the edge of the bed; he recognises the khaki trousers. This is it then. Without hesitation, he leans down and pulls the doll out by its leg. He transfers it to his other hand, clutching it around its waist, and stands back up. As he does so, he feels the rigid plastic underneath the doll's clothes begin to soften, become malleable. The doll wriggles to life in his palm...

His reaction is not that dissimilar to before. He gasps and lets go, dropping the doll on the bed in fright and repulsion. It bounces, then sits back up. 'Don't you ever do that to me again, Mr Lewis, walking out on me like that!' It looks up at him, its features softer again, more human; its eyes and mouth moving.

'You're ... you're alive!'

'Of course I'm alive, you touched me.'

'But ... I touched you before. I picked you up.'

'I know – *and* pulled my hair! I'd prefer it if you didn't do that actually; I'm quite partial to my hair. *And* you looked at my boobs.'

'I didn't!'

'You did. I didn't mind that so much, though.' This can't be happening. Not again, Mr Lewis thinks. He sits down on the bed, running his hands through his hair.

'But why didn't you come alive? Why now?'

'Because we have to be alone. Just me and you in the house. This is the first time it's happened since. When you leave I go back to normal. It's horrible, Mr Lewis. I don't mind if I can see a few things, you know, watch what's going on – or even the telly for that matter – but the last few days I've been stuffed down the end of the bed!' The doll stretches, arching its back and wriggling its bare toes; they all move individually, tiny digits with neat, clipped toenails.

'This can't be happening,' he says, putting his hands over his eyes. 'This simply can't be happening. You're not real.'

'Oh, I *am* real, Mr Lewis. Look!' The doll gets up and starts jumping up and down on the bed as if it's a trampoline, giggling and waving its arms about. It is most unnerving.

'Don't do that! Stop it!' says Mr Lewis.

'Why? I like it. I love to move! Weeeee!'

'Please stop! You're making my head spin, I can't think straight.' The doll slows down a bit, but doesn't stop. 'Listen to me. Are you saying that if I walk out of the house now you will go back to normal?' The doll stops suddenly and turns serious – just like that. It scrambles across the bed towards him. Mr Lewis jumps back.

'Oh please don't, Mr Lewis. Don't do that. Not yet. I've only just come alive! I'll be good, I promise. I'll do whatever you want.'

'I don't *want* you to do anything! Except go back to normal.'

'But this *is* normal, Mr Lewis. Being still and plastic and lifeless isn't normal.'

'You're a doll, for Christ's sake! And stop calling me Mr Lewis.'

'What do you want me to call you?'

'Nothing! I just want you to leave me alone. If you don't, I'll tell my wife.' As soon as he says it, he realises how ridiculous this sounds.

'Well, you could tell Mrs Lewis – nothing's stopping you. But what if she doesn't believe you?'

'Why wouldn't she believe me? What are you insinuating? I'll just make you come alive!'

'I'm not insinuating anything, Mr Lewis. And besides, it only works when we're on our own, remember?'

Shit, he'd forgotten that. 'Well, I'll just never pick you up again and that'll be that.'

'But you'll still know, won't you? Every time you put Lottie to bed. You'll still know that I can see and hear. I mean, it's up to you, Mr Lewis. It's your decision. I'll wait for you. I'll wait forever in case you change your mind, but it makes me sad to think of it...'

'Don't lay a guilt trip on me. How dare you! I'll just throw you out and be done with it!' Mr Lewis turns to storm out of the room, livid at being emotionally blackmailed by a doll.

But as he reaches the door he hears sobbing behind him. Quiet, human sobs. He turns round. The doll is sitting on the edge of the bed, biting its quivering lip, its little shoulders shaking in its khaki jacket, its long, calligraphy ink eyelashes matted and wet, crying the world's tiniest tears. It pains him. He's not a cruel man; he's a good man. But right now he feels like a big, mean monster. It confuses the hell out of him. 'I need time to think,' he says, closing the door behind him.

Mr Lewis puts the kettle on. He should be working, but can't even contemplate it. Instead, he paces the kitchen. The kettle boils. He doesn't want a coffee. His mouth is dry. What am I to do? What the hell am I to do? How can he possibly tell Dianne when he can never prove that what he's saying is true? He'd be carted off to the nuthouse. Realising this makes him feel trapped.

What if he *did* chuck the doll out? Would he really be able to go through with it – carrying the thing alive, kicking and screaming, to the bin? He shudders at the thought. And would it be fair on Lottie? It's her toy after all. What if he could contain it? Allow it out for maybe half an hour every Monday or something? He'd still be in control, wouldn't he? But where would it end? The longer it went on, and the more he conversed with the doll, the harder it would get. And then there was the guilt thing – seeing those tears. Why had they aroused such feelings of empathy in him? Perhaps it would be easier if it wasn't so pretty to look at – if it was bald, or fat, or ugly. Come on, they don't make dolls like that, do they?

After much vacillation, and a cup of coffee with a nip of brandy in it (this was becoming a dangerous habit), Mr Lewis heads back upstairs. His shoulders are stooped, as if he carries a heavy burden. As he turns the bedroom door handle, he wonders if the doll has turned back to plastic again. Part of him hopes this is the case, then he won't have to deal with it. He enters the room.

The doll is lying on its back, propped against a pillow, arms behind its head and its legs crossed. It turns and quickly sits up at Mr Lewis's arrival. It tidies its hair and wipes away any remaining tears with a little bit of tissue paper it has found from somewhere. 'Have you been thinking, Mr Lewis? Have you made a decision?'

Mr Lewis feels as if he should sit down on the bed whilst he discusses this, his fingers intertwined. It's a big decision, a serious matter. But he doesn't want to get too close to the thing in case it tries to touch him; he's not ready for that yet. 'I've decided to let you have a couple of hours' recreation time every Monday morning...'

'Oh, Mr Lewis!' the doll squeals, clapping its hands together. 'I could kiss you! You won't regret it, I promise.'

'Wait! I haven't finished. This arrangement is on a trial basis only, and under the proviso that you behave yourself. No monkey business. And needless to say, you shan't be able to leave this room.' The doll looks a little crestfallen. 'Well, we can't have you running about the house – I have work to do. Besides, you might get lost or something, or escape into the garden, heaven forbid. Or what if ... what if Dianne came back early? God, what am I doing...?' He trails off, rubbing his temples, the beginning of a migraine coming on again.

'No, that's fine, Mr Lewis. Thank you. You won't regret it.'

'No, I hope not. Now, I have work to do. So, no noise please.'

'I'll be as quiet as a mouse.'

Mr Lewis stands up. 'Oh, and one more thing. When I have to go out, which I have to in a couple of hours, you'll need to be put back where you were last. Otherwise it'll arouse suspicion.'

'But that means being shoved down the end of the bed!'

'Well, I'll sit you up the other way round or something. Look, it's not really my problem. I'm being more than fair. I don't know ... hopefully Lottie will play with you and leave you somewhere more interesting. Now, I really have to get on.'

Mr Lewis goes downstairs. He turns the computer on, feeling irresponsible because he hasn't done so already. The familiar screensaver greets him – a holiday snap: the three of them blissfully happy at Disneyland, Paris, with Woody from *Toy Story*. Lottie's toothless grin. Lord knows how they afforded it. The photo's a timely reminder. He's neglecting work, the lifeblood of the family. It's a dangerous game he's playing.

A drawn-out deal involving one of the most substantial residential properties in town is finally reaching its conclusion. The buyer, a cantankerous old bugger called Mr Gaunt (ironic considering how rotund he is), has been making endless demands and stipulations, trying to play hardball, and the vendors have dug in their heels. An impasse has been reached. To exacerbate matters, Gaunt will only deal with Mr Lewis himself; some customers are like that.

Mr Lewis feels like a negotiator caught between the two parties – repeating demands or trying to find compromises. All part of the job, unfortunately. But this one is a biggie, if it comes off. A selling price of £899,995 has been agreed in principle, so Lewis-Allen Estate Agents stands to earn around £11,000; they lower their commission rate to 1.25 per cent on properties over 500k. The vendors, the Simons, had wanted 1 per cent, but Mr Lewis had taken a risk on that one and stood firm.

And here he is, spending his morning talking to dolls. He decides to check his emails; hopefully there will be some good news. There's a bump from upstairs.

Mr Lewis stops and listens. No further sounds. She must have jumped down from the bed. She? The doll. He tries to concentrate again. Google Chrome, Hotmail, infuriating spinning circle thing ... what's it called? He'd looked it up once, but couldn't get to the bottom of it. Bloody computers. Bloody wi-fi. It's the same at work. Especially when they're all on at the same time – and always when you're on the phone to a customer and they're waiting for some important information: 'Sorry, Mrs so and so, the computer's being slow...' Cue awkward laugh, silence, heavy breathing; if he had a pound for every time that had happened...

There's a strange dragging sound across the floor above. What's the damn thing doing? He'd told it to be quiet. He listens again, straining his ears. There's the sound of thudding, rustling and rattling. It's right over his head, and the walls and floors are so thin: sometimes it sounds as if Lottie is going to come through when she jumps off her bed. There's a bang and a crash. The cat looks up, startled, its ears pricked and twitching. 'Right, that does it!'

Mr Lewis storms upstairs. He barges into the room.

'Look! This isn't going to work.' He stops. 'What on earth are you doing?' The doll has pulled a shoebox-sized metal tin, covered in camouflage-effect paint, across the floor. There are books stacked on top of it like steps, and the doll is now rummaging around in one of Lottie's plastic toy boxes – the stack type you get from pound shops. Toys, toy clothes, miniature things: everything's being chucked out onto the carpet.

'That blonde bimbo's got my dress!' says the doll over its shoulder.

'What blonde bimbo? What dress?'

'My blue gypsy dress with the flowers on it, the one I came in. Aha! There you are. Gotcha!' The doll starts yanking a bare plastic leg out of the pile of bric-a-brac, straining with the effort. Pretty soon a blonde doll appears, wearing a shiny blue dress as described. 'I've been wanting this back for ages,' she says, dumping the toy unceremoniously headfirst onto the floor.

Whilst Mr Lewis looks on, speechless, the doll clambers down and manhandles the blonde-haired doll on to its stomach. It puts its knee on the small of its back and proceeds to unbutton the dress from behind. It is the most bizarre sight he has ever seen in his life. It makes him feel faint. 'It never suited her anyway; Bimbo hasn't got the colouring for it, you see. Look at her, she's like a tangerine! But Lottie made us swap clothes. And I've had to put up with her cheap khaki outfit all these years, which chaffs in all the wrong places...'

This is too much information for Mr Lewis. 'Now look here. We had a deal. You were supposed to keep quiet. I'm trying to work and all I can hear is this commotion going on.'

'I'm sorry, Mr Lewis. I *will* be quiet – just as soon as I've got my dress back. Ugh!' The doll grunts as it yanks the dress down, leaving 'Bimbo' stranded naked on the floor. The doll turns, looking pleased and holding the dress up. Then, calm as you like, it proceeds to undo the buttons on the front of its jacket.

'God, no!' says Mr Lewis, holding up his hand and turning round. He knows there's nothing on under that jacket, and there's something not quite right about seeing the doll naked in its human form.

'Oh, sorry, Mr Lewis, I didn't mean to embarrass you. I won't be a minute.' There's an awkward wait whilst all that can be heard is the rustle of clothes against skin and the doll humming, totally unabashed. Mr Lewis concentrates on a scribble on the wall, tapping his foot and trying not to imagine anything. 'You *are* funny, Mr Lewis. Surely it's nothing you haven't seen before?'

'Will you please just hurry up and get dressed. I haven't got time for this.'

'Nearly done. There we go! You can turn round now. Will you help me with these buttons at the back?' Mr Lewis turns round slowly. The little doll is facing away from him, holding her sable black hair up to reveal her pale neck and back. The dress is satiny, royal blue with tiny white dots, tight at the waist and billowing at the hip. She's rotating her hips, swaying, waiting and humming again.

'No, I couldn't. I couldn't possibly. My fingers are way too big.'

'Spoilsport,' the doll says, reaching round and doing up all but one button, which is just out of reach. She turns back to face him. 'There,' she says, flicking her hair loose and flattening her dress. 'That's better. How do I look?' Mr Lewis says nothing. She looks pretty, though – too pretty; even with that slight gap in her teeth. It gives her an edge – the kind of thing a harlot would have in a period drama. It makes him feel strange.

'Can you please clear this mess up? Put everything back in the box – but quietly. I really have to work.' He sounds distracted, his voice lacking firmness or authority, as he turns to leave.

Things eventually calm down, and true to her word, the doll remains quiet for the rest of the morning. Feeling much more at ease, Mr Lewis manages to concentrate on work for a few hours. His thoughts don't return to the doll until he's making a sandwich for his lunch. He experiences a peculiar twinge of guilt. Does she get hungry? If so, what would she eat? Does she need the toilet? How old is she? Where did she come from? Does she feel pain? His thoughts are disturbed by his mobile going off. It's work. He needs to go in. Mr Gaunt is in and will only speak to him. Shit. Talk about timing. 'Give him a coffee and biscuits. Keep him happy. I'll be there in five.'

Mr Lewis slaps some cheese and tomatoes between slices of buttered bread, and without tidying up he heads for the door. He grabs his phone and reaches for his keys, putting his suit jacket on at the same time. Still trying to eat the sandwich, he locks the front door and gets in his car.

****

'Mr Gaunt. Good to see you.' There's a palpable silence in the office, save for Gaunt drumming his sausage fingers on the desk. Chantelle looks relieved to see her boss.

'Stephen,' says Mr Gaunt.

'Chantelle. Has Mr Gaunt had a coffee?' There's no evidence of this on the desk.

'He didn't want one, Mr Lewis.' Chantelle gives him a funny look, raising her eyebrows and scratching below her mouth. Mr Lewis pulls a confused face and ignores her, sitting down opposite his client.

'Now then, Mr Gaunt. What can we do for you today?'

'Well, I...' He stops, coughs and also gestures towards his chin, somewhat awkwardly. It dawns on Mr Lewis that he's got something stuck to his face. He quickly puts his hand to his chin, trying to brush the offending item away: tomato seeds, two of them. He blushes.

'Would you like a tissue?' Chantelle says, handing him one.

'Thank you. Sorry, I was just having my lunch.' He wipes his face and hands. 'Right. Where were we?'

It is as he listens to Mr Gaunt's latest demands, trying to look sympathetic and nodding his head at the right moments, that Mr Lewis starts thinking about the doll again. Mr Gaunt's voice drifts in and out of focus. He'd left the house without saying goodbye. The doll would be still again. More guilt. Why should I feel guilty? I'm not beholden to her. Where was she? Did she clean up the mess properly? What time is it? He tries to glance at his watch without Mr Gaunt noticing. One o'clock. An hour till his wife gets home. As long as he gets this meeting wrapped up he's got time to check – *and* clear that mess in the kitchen; Dianne hates it when he leaves a mess after his lunch. The dress. Oh God, the dress! The doll's still wearing the dress. Why hadn't he thought of that? 'Are you listening to me, Stephen?'

'Yes, yes. Of course.'

'So is that possible?'

'Possible?'

'To go and measure the drawing room for the dresser?'

'What, now?'

'Yes, now. If the dresser doesn't fit in the drawing room it could be a deal breaker. Mrs Gaunt is quite adamant about it.' This is typical of Gaunt: the property's already vacated and he's playing on this. Mr Lewis looks round at Chantelle. Owen is out on calls and Chantelle is the junior member of the team; she only answers the phones. Spends more time on her own phone, to be honest, which is exactly what she's doing now. Mr Gaunt follows his gaze. Chantelle looks up under the weight of their scrutiny. She puts her phone down and clicks on a mouse instead, trying to look busy. Mr Gaunt looks back at Mr Lewis with narrowed eyes.

'No problem, Mr Gaunt, but it'll have to be quick. I've got another viewing at two. Chantelle, can I have the keys to the Simon residence please?'

Three-quarters of an hour later, Mr Lewis is driving back home – too quickly. He's in a panic. That stupid old bastard had dragged it out as long as he could, snooping and asking questions, turning on taps, flushing toilets; the only thing he didn't do was take a dump in one of them. That was his third visit. Mr Lewis screeches into his drive, drawing a stare from his neighbour who is mowing his lawn. They both raise a hand in greeting as Mr Lewis dashes into the house.

Upstairs, he flings open Lottie's bedroom door. There's a loud bump as the door hits something. The doll rolls to a halt on her front in the middle of the carpet, her arms outstretched; he had just sent her flying. She's still lifeless and still wearing the dress. 'Oh God, sorry,' he says in his head. She must have been at the door when she heard him leave earlier. He picks her up, saying 'Eva, wake up!' and shaking her.

The doll wriggles to life in his hand. 'You said my name,' she says, a rapturous smile lighting up her face; he had, for the first time. He hadn't thought about it; it had just come out.

'Never mind that. You need to get changed, right now.'

'Why? Have you changed your mind about watching me get undressed?'

'Listen! I haven't got time for your games,' he says, squeezing her. 'You need to get changed back into your other outfit. My wife will be home any minute.' It occurs to him how wrong this sounds out loud.

'There's no need to squeeze the life out of me! You only have to ask nicely,' the doll says, placing her hands on his fingers and trying to lever some breathing room.

'Just do it!' he says, placing her on the floor.

'OK. Pass me Bimbo, then,' she says, placing her hands on her hips.

'Where is she? I mean, *it*?'

'Back in the box where she belongs.' Mr Lewis groans and stomps over to the plastic purple box. He grabs the blonde doll. It's naked.

'Where's her bloody outfit?' he shouts.

'It's in there somewhere, the horrible old thing.' Mr

Lewis ferrets around desperately until he finds the little jacket and trousers. He can't believe his life has come to this. He extracts them both and strides across the room with them to Eva. The clothes look tiny in his hands. Eva giggles.

'What's so funny?' he says, unamused.

'Nothing.'

'Just get on with it!'

'All right, Mr Bossy Boots. Turn around then – unless you *want* to watch this time!' Mr Lewis finds himself hesitating before turning round. Again, he tries to make his mind go blank as he hears rustling. It seems to be taking an age. He looks at his watch. It's ten to two. Shit. 'I like it when you hold me, Mr Lewis. It feels nice. Not when you're squeezing me half to death, though. You don't know how strong you are.' Mr Lewis doesn't know how to answer this. She never shuts up.

'Please, just hurry up!'

'Right, all done. You can turn around now. God, I hate this outfit.' The doll is back in the khaki jacket and trousers, pouting and looking grumpy.

'Right, get the dress back on Bimbo and put her back in the box. Then get back on the bed – or wherever you were this morning. I've got to go and tidy the kitchen.' God, how did this become so normal so quickly? They were like partners in crime. He moves towards the door. Suddenly there's a stomach-churning sound – the front door opening. Mr Lewis freezes.

'Hi! Are you home?' Dianne; she's early. He hears keys being hung up and the front door closing. Oh shit, oh shit, oh shit! Mr Lewis looks across the bedroom. Eva is flat on her back on the floor. The other doll is next to her still, minus its dress. '*Stephen?*' He screws up his face, wanting to cry. Oh God, I'm having a mental breakdown. He chomps down on his bottom lip, screwing his eyes tight shut and praying. There's the familiar sound of her coat and bag being hung on the bottom banister post; her normal routine. If she comes up the stairs now he's screwed – his marriage could be over. He holds his breath, sweat popping out on his forehead…

He hears her go from the lounge to the kitchen. Still he doesn't move a muscle. 'Oh, wonderful!' she says. Shit. He never got to clear up. The pipe in the bathroom jolts as she turns on the cold tap, making him jump. He hears the kettle being slammed back into its cradle. Then he hears the other tap come on and the rattle of pots in the sink. Wait … wait … not yet. When the kettle begins to whistle, he decides to make a move. Crouching, his knees cracking all too loudly, he picks up the two dolls and the dress, then tiptoes out of the room with them, across the landing and to the safety of his and his wife's bedroom.

His plan is to wait till Dianne goes to pick Lottie up from school, dress the other bloody doll, then put them both back where they belong. But where does he hide them in the meantime? He scans the room. Somewhere high; the top of the wardrobe, under the suitcases.

Mission accomplished, he messes up his hair and heads down stairs. He gets about halfway when his wife calls, 'Stephen? Is that you?'

'Yes, sorry. I was having a lie down.'

'God. You gave me a fright! I thought you'd walked into work. Didn't you hear me calling you?' He reaches the bottom of the stairs. Mrs Lewis is in the lounge.

'Well, I thought I heard something. That's probably what woke me up. I had the earphones in and must have drifted off.'

'You look terrible. You're all clammy. Are you feeling all right?'

'No. That's why I had a lie down. Had one of my migraines coming on.'

'This is becoming a regular thing on a Monday. I hope it's not stress. Have you been in?'

'Yes. Gaunt wanted to see me.'

'Oh, any news?' Mrs Lewis looks hopeful.

'Not really, I'm afraid. More demands. Another viewing. He still seems keen enough, though. Do you want a cup of tea?'

'Oh, I'll make it.'

'No, I'll do it. You sit down. I'll tidy up this lot.' He kisses Mrs Lewis and gives her a hug. 'Sorry about the mess. I was called in suddenly and then this migraine came on. I was going to do it before you came back and then I dozed off. I don't know where the day's gone.'

****

Putting the dolls back wasn't as straightforward as he'd envisaged. He'd totally forgotten Eva was going to come alive again, as the house was empty. It gave him a fright. 'You could have put me in a nicer place, Mr Lewis. It was dusty and dark up there, and I'm sure I heard a spider crawling about.'

'I'm not listening to you. You've got me in enough trouble today. Just be quiet and go back to sleep.' Eva tries to engage him in conversation further as he dresses the blonde doll, but he doesn't take any notice; he's had enough of her incessant patter for one day. He chucks Bimbo back in the box and places Eva at the end of the bed.

'Face up, remember,' she says.

'I know. You don't need to tell me. Now stay there and don't get up.' He leaves the room without looking back. Then he has to leave the house to make her go to sleep. It's ridiculous. He pretends to search for something in his car so it doesn't look strange. When he re-enters the house he goes back upstairs to check. Eva is still in place. Thank the Lord for small mercies. 'Never again,' he says to himself as he closes the door. As he walks away, it occurs to him that she would have heard him.

CHAPTER 4

'Never again'. A phrase often uttered, but rarely adhered to. Whether it be an alcoholic with a chronic hangover, a gambler after a heavy loss, a binge-eater after a blow out or a smoker who says 'Once this pack's finished, I'm quitting', there usually *is* an 'again'. The boredom soon kicks in, the addiction, the habit. You realise that the thing you're starving yourself of is the most exciting thing you've got in your life.

With Mr Lewis, this takes the grand total of five hours or so. Make no mistake, he'd meant it at the time when he'd said it: the day had spiralled out of control – something he never wanted to go through again. But when he's trying to watch telly that night little things keep coming back to him; that feeling of danger and excitement. Eva's voice, her playfulness, her flattery, the things she says: 'I like it when you hold me, Mr Lewis, it feels nice.'

The thing is, it had felt nice to him too. It had awoken dormant, primal feelings in him, reminded him

Eva: A grown-up fairy tale

of watching *King Kong* as a child – the original; the scene when Fay Wray's wrists are tied to the posts – the offering, the sacrifice – the ultimate damsel in distress in a slip of a dress, flesh on display – the pounding of the drums. How tiny she had looked in Kong's hand. He could have crushed the life out of her but he didn't. He was tender with her. He loved her. This profoundly affected Mr Lewis as a boy on a level he couldn't possibly understand. And this felt the same somehow.

He's fully aware of Eva when he's putting Lottie to bed that night, just as she said he would be; knowing she can hear, knowing she can see. He tries not to look at her. This feeling goes on all week. Twice he has the opportunity to touch her, to wake her up – once when Dianne takes Lottie to swimming club, and again when they go supermarket shopping together: Lottie always insists on going – Lord knows what the fascination is; probably the possibility of a treat. But he resists, fearful of the can of worms he could open up; something he can't put back in time. Pandora's box; oh, Eva was that all right. The fear he felt when Dianne came home that Monday, when he was stuck in Lottie's bedroom, is still fresh in his mind.

The following Monday morning arrives like a delayed package ordered online – long overdue and eagerly awaited. Mr Lewis runs straight upstairs after seeing his family off. He picks Eva up, anticipating the now familiar give of her body, with a look of boyish expectancy on his face. 'Eva, wake up. It's Monday!' There's nothing: no softening, no movement. 'Eva, wake up!' He shakes her, not understanding. Still nothing – just her wide, blank, brown eyes staring out at him. 'What the hell?' He moves one of her arms up and down, a rising panic in his belly. 'Eva!' He strokes her hair, desperate. What's happened? Why isn't she waking up?

Suddenly she blinks, her long lashes opening and closing like a pair of blinds on two sad little chocolate windows.

'What?' she says, her body finally softening but her voice cold.

'Oh God. Thank God. Don't ever do that to me again!' He feels like pressing her to him.

'Why not? You deserve it, you big horrible man! I thought you meant it when you said "never again".' She begins to beat his hand with her tiny fists, and sobs. 'Have you any idea what I've been going through?' She continues to slap him: it feels like the beating of a butterfly's wings.

'I'm sorry. I'm truly sorry,' Mr Lewis says, gently putting her down on the bed. 'I didn't mean it. I was stressed out. Here, let me get you a tissue.' He reaches over to the chest of drawers and grabs a fresh tissue out of a cellophane pack. He rips a little corner off it, the size he'd put over a shaving cut, and passes it to her. It's like a full-sized hanky in her hands. He watches as she dabs her eyes and blows her nose, her chest and shoulders jerking. She looks up with the tissue still over her nose.

'Oh, don't look at me,' she says nasally. 'I must look awful.'

'Don't be silly.'

'Gross,' she says, inspecting the tissue, as if what she sees in it is a surprise. This makes Mr Lewis wonder what else she does. She cries real tears; she gets a snotty nose. Does she bleed? Does she sweat? She is more and more intriguing all the time. He waits until she's calmed down. Her little face is puffy from crying.

'Eva?'

'Yes, Mr Lewis.'

'Why didn't you wake up straightaway? I don't understand.'

'I delayed it on purpose,' she says, giving her eyes one last wipe with the back of her hand.

'What, you can do that?'

'Apparently so. I didn't know myself until then. I'm full of tricks, it seems. I wanted to teach you a lesson. I'm sorry.'

'Well, it worked.'

'Good.' A sheepish smile returns to her face. It's good to see. Mr Lewis hesitates for a moment, as if debating something.

'Look, I've got an idea. Why don't you come downstairs with me, just for a little while? I know it's against the rules, but I guess it won't hurt for a bit.' He still feels bad and wants to cheer her up – a little treat. Not only that; it's starting to feel a little uncomfortable doing all this in his daughter's bedroom. It doesn't feel right.

'Really?' Her face lights up and she stands up excitedly, clapping her hands together.

'Yes. Not for too long, though. And you'll have to be quiet. I've got work to do, remember.' He tries to sound serious, but has to suppress a smile at her glee.

'You know me, Mr Lewis. Good as gold! Can I wear my dress?' she says, slipping down from the bed.

'No, we haven't got time for that.' Eva looks disappointed.

'Well, at least let a girl put some shoes on – the floor hurts my feet.' Mr Lewis groans. 'I won't be a minute.' She runs over to the camouflage tin again and starts dragging it across the floor.

'Look, it'll be a lot quicker if I do it. We can't have you piling books up again. We'll be here all day.' He walks over to the toy box, grabs hold of Bimbo and quickly pulls her shoes off. 'Here,' he says.

'God, they're no good. They'll keep falling off; Bimbo's got man-feet. *My* feet are dainty.'

Mr Lewis lets out a huff of exasperation. 'What, then?'

'My shoes will be in there somewhere. They're white. Wedges.' Mr Lewis has no idea what wedges are. He starts rummaging about in the box. Eva stands on the metal tin, jumping up and down, but it's no good. 'Hold me up, Mr Lewis, I can't see.'

'I can't hold you and sort through the box, can I?' He's starting to regret this.

'Well, sit me on the edge then.' He picks Eva up, her jacket shifting against her tiny waist, and puts her on the corner of the box. 'That's better,' she says. She oversees proceedings by leaning forward, whilst keeping her balance with both hands. 'Try at the bottom. Pull everything out.'

'I am!' The bottom of the box becomes visible. Glitter, coins, Lego bricks, stray puzzle pieces.

'There's one!' she cries. A little off-white shoe, covered in dust, appears amongst the junk. Mr Lewis extracts it and hands it over. She blows on it, then clutches it to her chest like an old friend. As he continues to search, Eva pops the shoe on; he can see it out of the corner of his eye, dangling over the box as he sweeps the junk from side to side. After what seems like several minutes, rooting around on his knees, he finds the other shoe. 'Oh thank you, Mr Lewis. Thank you. I haven't worn these for ages!' He puts her back down and shoves everything back in the box.

Meanwhile Eva is tilting her calves up in turn, admiring her shoes. 'These are the ones I came in, you see. They really don't go with this silly outfit, though.'

'Where *did* you come from?' Mr Lewis asks.

'A car-boot stall. Lottie picked me out. I'm glad she did, otherwise I'd never have met you. I only cost a pound! Pretty cheap, don't you think? Just because I'm not a fancy make.'

'But I meant originally. Where were you made?'

'Spain.'

'So why don't you speak Spanish?'

'Because I couldn't hear then; I hadn't unlocked it. I've only ever heard English. Everything I've ever learnt is from English telly, songs or people.' Mr Lewis silently marvels at this.

'And how old are you meant to be?'

'All these questions, Mr Lewis. I don't have an age, do I? I wasn't born, I was just made. I didn't grow up and I'll never get old – I'm "*all woman*" if that's what you mean!' She strikes a pose as if to demonstrate this, one hand on her hip and the other pushing her hair up, lips pouting.

'Yes, quite,' says Mr Lewis, coughing. 'Well, come on if you're coming.' He gestures with his head. She follows him across the room, skipping. It's a strange sight. Almost as if he's taking a pet for a walk.

As he starts to descend the stairs he notices she's not following any more. He turns to see her still on the landing, looking uncertain. 'I'm not sure about the stairs, Mr Lewis. It looks a long way down. I've never been down stairs before. Will you carry me?' Mr Lewis drops to his knees, his face almost level with hers. He scoops her up and she snuggles into his hand as he carries her downstairs. 'Woah! Not too fast. It makes my tummy go funny!'

He rounds the bottom of the stairs into the lounge, laughing, when all of a sudden the front door rattles and bangs. In a knee-jerk reaction of blind panic, Mr Lewis flings the doll onto the sofa and stands there, guilt etched all over his face. Through the glass of the porch door, he sees a bundle of post flop onto the floor. The letter box snaps shut again. 'Jesus Christ!' he says, holding his heart and leaning on the banister. 'I thought that was Dianne. Look, this isn't going to work; it was a bad idea. You're going to have to go back upstairs.'

'Oh, don't worry about me!' Eva says, clambering gingerly to her knees. 'You nearly broke my arm!' She tries to bend it.

'I doubt that's even possible…' Suddenly there's a low growl. They both turn towards it. There on the other sofa is the cat with its fur raised, tail and all. It crouches low, chin flat to the sofa, eyes wide and trained on one thing: Eva. It growls again. Eva screams. The sound is shrill and loud – loud for something so tiny anyway. The cat's hindquarters begin to wiggle, ready to pounce. Its claws come out.

'Stella! No!' Mr Lewis shouts. He intercepts the cat just in time, smacking it away. The cat lets out a yelp and scarpers, making for the back door. The cat flap bangs.

To Mr Lewis's surprise Eva's turned back into a doll; it must have been the shock. He wakes her up, and she immediately scrambles up his arm, a look of sheer terror on her face. She clambers all the way to the top, then flings herself around his neck, trembling and clinging on like a baby koala. 'Oh, Mr Lewis, take me back upstairs! I don't like it here,' she wails. She nuzzles into him, trying to hide, which makes a rasping sound on his stubble. He can feel the rapid, rabbit-foot pounding of her tiny heart against his throat. Her hair tickles him and she has no discernible smell.

'It's OK,' he says. 'She's gone outside. It's only Stella.' He tries to pull her off, but she holds on tighter.

'Only Stella! That thing's a monster. It wants to eat me!'

'Well, she probably thought you were a mouse or something.' But he suddenly realises how terrifying it must have been for her. The cat was ten times her size, or more. It must have looked like a mutant grizzly bear. 'I'll lock her out. Don't worry. Now if you'll just let go a minute.' Mr Lewis tries to pull her away again.

'Don't put me down. Please. Carry me in your hand.'

'OK, OK, if you'll just let go.' Eva finally relinquishes her grip and he transfers her to his hand, where she tries to make herself as small and inconspicuous as possible. He walks through the kitchen and into the utility room. Reaching the back door, he pushes the guard down on the cat flap, locking it for good measure.

'Are you sure it can't get in?' comes a muffled voice from his hand.

'Yes, quite sure.' She pops her head out for the first time.

'Where are we?' she says. 'It smells in here.'

'That's probably Stella's food bowls.'

'Ugh. It's disgusting.'

'So you can smell?'

'Yes. I figured that out a while ago. *You* smell nice, Mr Lewis; especially your neck.'

'Oh, you're getting back to normal again,' he says, smiling.

'I feel a whole lot better now that monster's gone.'

'Do you still want to go back upstairs?'

'No. Put me on the side, Mr Lewis, I'm getting too hot. Your hand's wet.'

'Oh, sorry.' He places her on the side in the kitchen, her legs dangling over the edge. Some of her hair is sticking to her forehead from the damp, just as a human's would. She brushes it aside and leans forward to peer down.

'Woah! That was a bad idea. I don't think I like it up here – not on the edge. It's different when I'm in your hand, I feel safe.' Again, Mr Lewis tries to imagine some sort of comparison: sitting up there on the kitchen counter would to her be like sitting on the top of a house to him. She clambers to the back of the work surface and sits with her back against the tiles, next to a double plug socket. 'What do *these* do?' she says, sticking her hand in a hole.

'God, no! Don't do that!' he says, lunging forward and grabbing her little arm. 'You'll electrocute yourself.'

'Ow! That's my sore arm. What does electrocute mean?'

Eva: A grown-up fairy tale

'It means … it means, well, basically it would fry you. You'd be dead.' It was a stark reminder of the danger that was all around for a tiny person; especially one so naive. It was like having a toddler in the house again.

Up close, he can see a red bloom on one of her cheeks. It looks like a rash, a reaction to his stubble. He pushes her clingy ebony hair aside with his finger to see better. His fingernail practically covers her cheek. She looks up at this surprisingly tender touch.

'You really do feel, don't you?' he says. 'You're a miracle.'

'I certainly am, Mr Lewis.'

He falters for a moment. He's at a loss. This is all too much. How can he begin his day with her down here? He must try. Start with a coffee. That usually works. He fills the kettle and switches it on. Another danger. Eva watches.

'Right. I'm going to put you back in the lounge: it's safer in there. I've got to make a phone call. Just sit on the sofa for a minute and don't do anything. Don't touch anything.' He carries her through to the lounge.

'Ugh, no! Not on that one. It's covered in that monster's hairs,' she says, clinging to his hand. He puts her on the larger sofa. She inspects it, pacing around before finding a satisfactory spot. Fussy little thing.

Mr Lewis tries to clear his mind. Right. I've got to call the office. He hasn't switched the computer on yet. Where's my phone? Jesus, where's my phone? 'Eva, have you seen my phone?'

'It's on the side in the kitchen,' she says. He looks. It is. Hmm, useful. It's like having his own miniature personal secretary. Shame she can't make coffee. He calls the office, pushing the button on the computer at the same time.

'Hi Chantelle, it's Stephen ... fine, thank you. How was your weekend? Good. Can you just check the diary for me, see what we've got today?' He looks over at Eva. She's watching him intently. 'Nothing at all? Oh, right. Tomorrow? ... OK, just two. And the rest of the week? Well, it's only Monday: you know what it's like, things can change. Anything from Gaunt? I haven't checked my emails yet... OK, keep me posted. I'll be at home. If anything major changes I'll come in, otherwise I probably won't bother. Is Owen in yet? Tell him to go through the database – prepare a mailshot. We've got to be proactive. He knows what to do. OK, see you later. Bye.' Mr Lewis ends the call. He looks depressed.

'Who's Chantelle?' comes a little voice.

'Oh, she's just a girl from the office.'

'Do you fancy her?'

'What? No! What sort of question is that? I'm married. She's not my type anyway.'

'What is your type?'

'I don't have a type. It's just an expression.'

'Is Mrs Lewis your type? Do you fancy *her*?' Eva giggles.

'You really shouldn't be asking these questions.' Mr Lewis walks back into the kitchen, blushing; a grown man reduced to a flustered teenager by an eleven inch doll.

'Oh, so it's all right for *you* to ask questions!' He ignores her.

Mr Lewis makes his coffee, then returns to the lounge to sit at his desk. Eva clambers up to the back of the sofa, where she can sit and watch him. 'Oh, can I watch telly with you, Mr Lewis?'

'I'm not watching telly: this is a computer. That's a monitor.'

'You mean like Lottie's tablet?'

'Sort of. And it's not *Lottie's* tablet.'

'Oh right. I did wonder. Sometimes I hear swear words on it.'

'What do you mean?' Mr Lewis says, suddenly taking more interest.

'Nothing.'

'Eva, tell me!' His voice is firm.

'Well, sometimes she watches movie clips with swear words in them. I can't see them, just hear them.'

'Oh, does she now? And what else does she watch?'

'Mostly animal clips: you know, pets doing silly things. She laughs at them. Music videos too. That's all.'

'Hmm,' says Mr Lewis, rubbing his chin. This has been an interesting conversation – a miniature secretary *and* a spy.

'Lottie's not in trouble, is she?'

'No, no,' says Mr Lewis. 'Now, I really have to concentrate.'

'Well, what shall *I* do?'

'I don't know. Why don't you explore or something? Actually, no – that's a bad idea. God knows what trouble you'll get into.'

'Can I watch the big telly?' she asks. Mr Lewis considers this. It could be a distraction. At least it was safe and might shut her up for a bit.

'OK. But you'll have to keep the sound down.' He gets up and turns on the telly with the remote. He turns it down to a barely audible level and puts the remote on the sofa next to her. It's not much smaller than she is.

'Wow! That telly's huge!' Eva cries.

'Now, you have to press this button to change channels...'

'I know what to do, Mr Lewis. Lottie's got a telly, remember.'

'Oh yes. Of course.' She begins to push the change channel button down with the palm of her little hand. It's a truly amazing sight. Mr Lewis shakes his head. He tries to concentrate on his computer screen, tries to focus, but keeps getting distracted by Eva flicking through the channels.

'Why don't you just choose something?' he says.

'I thought you were meant to be working.'

'I am.' Eventually, she settles on a shopping channel. Her choices fascinate him.

'It's nice to be able to watch what I want for a change ... ooh, I like that dress!' she remarks. 'All Lottie watches is cartoons. Or the music channels. I like those, though. Which one's the sound button?'

'Just leave it.' She finds it and turns the volume up anyway. 'That's far enough!' It's like dealing with a naughty child.

'All right, Mr Grumpy Pants.'

After going through his emails and replying to a few, Mr Lewis, as he often does, strays onto rival estate agents' websites. He feels the usual bitter stab of envy when he sees 'SOLD STC' stamped across properties, or the nearly as bad 'UNDER OFFER' captions. What are they doing that he isn't? They'd signed up with all the big internet property sales sites now; something they'd put off for as long as possible.

It's all right for his more or less silent partner, David, who's an old friend: he has his work on the side. He's a fully qualified property surveyor – and because this is a service Lewis-Allen offers he'd come on board – 60/40 in Mr Lewis's favour, bringing a much-needed injection of cash for some new office equipment. When sales are good it works in Mr Lewis's favour. But when things go quiet David has his freelance work to fall back on, lucky sod.

Maybe an open house or two is the thing – get people through some doors. He just needs to pick the right properties – presentable ones. No wonder some of the houses don't sell: filthy carpets, black mould round windows, rooms stinking of dogs. And then when the owners get a reduced offer they take umbrage. Refuse to accept it. It's maddening.

Out of the corner of his eye, he notices Eva has dropped down from the sofa, obviously bored with the telly. She seems to have found something more interesting on the other side of the room, and is making a beeline for a wooden chest. She stands, staring at it, with her head cocked to the side. 'Ugh!' she says. 'You know you've got beetles crawling over this chest?'

'They're ants,' he says, going back to the screen. 'We get them every year. They get drawn to the fruit bowl.'

'Ants? They're huge.' She slinks towards him; there's something feline about her – although she'd hate him for thinking it. 'Can I watch you for a bit? See what you're doing?' He looks down at her, a little annoyed at the constant interruptions. She looks back up at him, batting her eyelids and smiling, her lips as red as Snow White's apple and probably as dangerous.

'If you promise to be quiet.' She holds up her arms to be picked up. Mr Lewis pops her on the desk next to him. She stares up at the screen for a while.

'That doesn't look very exciting.'

'It's not meant to be exciting; it's work,' he replies curtly.

'Doesn't it hurt your eyes? It hurts mine,' she says, turning away. He ignores her. She lies on her side next to his hand, propped on one elbow – like a cat again, trying to get noticed, hoping for a tummy rub. It doesn't work. She sighs, examining his giant hand hovering above the mouse, his huge wristwatch, the hairs on his wrist. She starts running her fingers through them. It tickles him and he twitches. 'You're so big, Mr Lewis.'

'Do you mind? I'm trying to work!' He grabs her and pops her onto the floor.

'Sorry!' she says, put out. She saunters over to the patio doors onto the garden, puts her hands up against the glass and stares out. The cat is sulking on a bench. It hasn't seen her. She thumbs her nose at it.

'I wish I could go outside,' she says wistfully. 'Not with that beast out there, obviously, but, you know, with you.'

Mr Lewis turns from his computer. He might as well give up. 'I thought you said you *had* been outside, on holiday with us?'

'Yes, I know. But I wasn't awake then. I couldn't move. I want to feel the grass on my legs, the sun on my face, to smell the flowers. Do you think it would work – the magic? When you leave the house I go back to normal, same if there's other people about. I wonder what would happen if you took me outside and there was no one else there?'

'I don't know. It's too risky. What would a grown man be doing with a doll in his garden?'

'Well, you could sneak me out there. Put me in the long grass.'

'I don't know about that. What if someone saw? That reminds me actually. What was so funny about that holiday in Cornwall? I remember you laughing at something.' Mr Lewis turns round in his chair, leaning down.

'Oh, nothing. Just me being silly, that's all.' Eva is smiling again, coyly, revelling in the glow of his full attention.

'You can't just say that. Clearly something amused you. Come on, tell me.'

'Well, you probably didn't notice at the time, but for a few days I got left in the open suitcase on the floor in your bedroom.'

'And? Oh my God! What did you see? Please tell me you were facing the other way! We had an en-suite shower room at that cottage!' His mind is rapidly turning over. Hadn't they been trying for another baby then? Enthusiastically...

'I didn't actually *see* anything, more's the pity, so you can relax.'

'Phew! Thank God for that. Well what then? What's the big deal?'

'I still heard things, though.'

'Oh no.' Mr Lewis covers his face with his hands.

'You and Mrs Lewis ... morning *and* night!'

'Oh God,' he groans.

'Sounded like you were both enjoying yourselves, especially Mrs Lewis. She can't half swear when she wants to, can she?'

'OK, that's enough.' Having his sex life scrutinised and commented on by a doll is a step too far.

'It made me feel funny…'

'I said *enough*!' He looks up as he chastises her, but she's already staring out of the window into the garden again. She looks serious for once.

CHAPTER 5

Trying to work with Eva around is nigh on impossible. She's going to have go back upstairs soon. Mr Lewis gets up from his desk, but leaves the computer on. It's only mid-morning but he's feeling peckish already – probably because he was too excited to eat any breakfast first thing; how ridiculous is that? 'I'm going to make myself something to eat, and then you'll have to go back upstairs, I'm afraid.'

'Already? But I've only been down here for an hour or so. Mrs Lewis isn't back till two. I've been looking forward to this all week!'

'You don't have to go back to sleep. You can still do what you like upstairs – as long as you're quiet, that is.'

'But...'

'No buts, Eva. I mean it. I can't get anything done whilst you're around.'

'Why? Do I distract you?'

'Yes, you do!' He walks into the kitchen and Eva

pads after him, her lips pursed in a mischievous, satisfied smile.

'What are you having to eat, Mr Lewis? What's it like to eat? Can I watch you?' She follows him out to the fridge freezer in the utility room.

'Do you ever stop asking questions?' he says, opening the fridge and peering in.

'No. I want to know everything. I'm like a sponge. Can I look in the fridge too?'

'Why would you want to look in a fridge?'

'I want to feel how cold it is. I've never felt a real fridge. Lottie's got a play one – and a cooker – for spoilt brat Bimbo, but they don't work.'

Mr Lewis turns round and picks her up. He places her on a shelf next to a low-fat yoghurt, sitting down and facing him.

'Ooh, God, these bars are freezing!' she says. 'Put me in the door!'

'You ought to try the freezer then,' he says, standing her in the door rack next to a squeezy mayonnaise bottle. It comes up to her shoulder. She leans on the plastic barrier like a fence, watching him as he pulls out various food items – the salad box, a block of cheese, the spread, the mayonnaise. 'Don't forget me!' she says.

Her voice becomes muffled as he closes the door on her. Her face is a picture as it swings shut in front of his eyes. He hears her scream as he walks back into the kitchen, his arms full of food. He smiles to himself, pleased at his little joke; there's something about her that brings out the child in him.

He bundles his stuff on the worktop, then goes back to retrieve her, still smiling. She's pummelling on the door and shouting. He opens it, but carefully, just in case she falls out. 'You horrible, horrible man!' she shouts, turning round. 'That wasn't funny. It was dark in there, and cold!' She pummels his hand as he picks her up. This just makes him laugh more. 'Ooh, that tickles,' he says, teasing her. 'You said you wanted to know what a real fridge felt like. Now you know.'

'You're mean!' she says, biting his hand instead. It feels more like a pinch, not really painful.

'That still doesn't hurt, you know. Go on, try harder,' he says, chuckling. This makes her even madder. Eva chomps down on his skin, grinding her teeth, sinking in an incisor. This time it does hurt.

'Ow! You little minx!' he cries, pulling her off with his other hand and shaking the bitten one. There are miniature bite marks on it, and she's drawn blood. He holds her up in the air by her jacket so that she's dangling by it, thrashing about. It reminds him of the film *One Million Years B.C.*, when the pterodactyl carries Raquel Welch off to its nest. This gives him an idea. He wonders if Bimbo's got a spare fur bikini anywhere. Eva would look rather fetching in that. 'Careful or I'll drop you, wild thing.'

'Well, you told me to bite harder!'

'Does that mean we're even?'

'No. You're a big bully!' But she's smiling now, and has stopped fighting.

'Can I put you down?'

'Please do.' He pops her on the tiled window sill, next to the little digital radio. She straightens her jacket and tidies her hair. There's a glow to her cheeks, as if she's enjoyed their little play fight. Then she pulls a face and opens her mouth, licking the back of her hand. It leaves a red smear.

'What's wrong?' he asks.

'I've got this horrible taste in my mouth. I think it's your blood. Ugh.' She keeps opening and closing her mouth, shaking her hands and pulling a face. 'I can't get rid of it.'

'Do you want a drink to wash it away?'

'I don't know. I've never had a drink before.' Mr Lewis looks around for something to use as a receptacle. Everything's too big.

'Bimbo's got some cups,' she says. Mr Lewis dashes upstairs. He returns some moments later with a little opaque, turquoise, plastic cup. He puts it under the tap. It only holds a few drops. He passes it to her, impossibly tiny in his fingers. Eva hesitates.

'I'm not sure, Mr Lewis. What if I'm not meant to drink? What if something happens?'

'Like what?'

'I don't know. What if it poisons me, or just pours straight out of some holes?'

'You look pretty human to me in every way. Your heart beats, you can smell and taste. Surely you've got to get thirsty. Especially the longer you're awake. Hungry too, no doubt.'

'Well, here goes. It's been nice knowing you, Mr Lewis.' She takes an experimental sip and gulps. Her throat bobs up and down. Mr Lewis waits with baited breath, suddenly feeling a little anxious. Heaven forbid anything should happen to her.

'It tastes strange. It feels cold inside me,' she says. 'I can feel it trickling down.' Nothing extraordinary happens. She waits for a moment then takes another sip. 'It's all right once you get used to it, I suppose. At least it's taken that taste away. 'She passes the cup back. 'Here. I'd better not overdo it. Thank you.'

'So you won't be biting me again in a hurry?'

'I didn't say that. I just won't draw blood next time! Your skin tasted all right.'

'Oh. That's good to know.' Mr Lewis proceeds to make his lunch in front of her, buttering two slices of bread. He's got to admit he's got used to her being around; he kind of likes the company – it's better than the cat – and even the prattle. He presses the 'on' switch on the radio. Music blares out, making Eva jump and cover her ears. 'Shit. Sorry.' He turns it down.

'Jesus, you frightened me to death. My ears have gone funny.' She tries to unblock them with her fingers.

'Do you want me to turn it off?'

'No, I love music. Just not that loud.'

The radio is permanently tuned to an '80s station, and Mr Lewis is soon singing along to Spandau Ballet's 'Gold'. This makes Eva giggle. 'I've never seen you singing before,' she says, nodding her head to the music. Up next is 'Mickey' by Toni Basil. Eva jumps up. 'Oh, I love this one!' she cries.

'Same here. How do you know it?'

'I must hear it at least three times a week. Lottie watches it on her tablet. She likes the video. So do I.'

'Ah. That's my girl. The '80s music has rubbed off on her then. You know more about my daughter than I do.' Lottie was still at that blissful age before she'd started forming her own tastes – when a child just likes what she likes without questioning it – mainly based on her parents' influence. She'd sing along to anything from Dolly Parton to Foo Fighters. None of this modern pop rubbish.

Eva starts doing all the dance moves to the 'Mickey' video, prancing about on the windowsill like a miniature cheerleader with imaginary pompoms, clapping and pointing to Mr Lewis; his own personal performance. He feels a little embarrassed by all the attention. Still, it's not every day you get serenaded whilst making your brunch, he thinks.

'Right, that's enough music,' he says, turning it off. He's finished making his sandwich.

'Oh! I was enjoying that.'

'Yes, a little too much.' Her face is properly flushed.

'Did you want something to eat before I pack this away? Are you hungry?'

'How do you know if you're hungry?'

'I don't know. You have a pain in your belly, I suppose.'

'A pain?'

'Well, not a pain, but it feels slightly uncomfortable, rumbles, makes noises.'

'Oh. Maybe then. I wondered what that was. It's like the longer I'm awake and the more I move about, the more I can feel it.'

'Yep. You're hungry. Here, try some bread.' He rips a tiny soft bit of bread from the middle of his sandwich and hands it to her.

'But what do I do? Just swallow it like the water?'

'Try chewing it first. You don't want it to get stuck.'

'Stuck? What, forever?'

'No. Look, just take your time. I'll get some more

water for you to wash it down with.' She takes the bread, looking at it mistrustfully. It seems such an alien concept to her: to put something in her mouth and swallow it. Where will it go to? What will happen to it? Mr Lewis fills the tiny cup again and places it next to her.

'After three,' he says. 'One...'

'No, wait. I'm too scared. Water first – so it slips down easier.' She takes a gulp of water.

'OK. One, two, three.'

She shoves the morsel in and closes her eyes, screwing up her face and chomping before quickly swallowing it. 'More water, more water.' She gulps it down.

'How was that?'

'Weird.'

Mr Lewis gathers everything up to put back in the fridge, then says, 'I'm just nipping out for a pee; I'll be back in a minute.'

'Ooh! Can I watch?'

'No! That's too weird. You can't watch everything, you know. Stay here.' Mr Lewis closes the downstairs toilet door, just in case. He's mid-pee when he hears a voice on the other side of the door.

'Gosh, Mr Lewis. It sounds like a waterfall!'

'Jesus Christ! How did you get down?'

'I climbed down the metal drawer handles. It didn't seem so far down after being up in that fridge.' Mr Lewis flushes the toilet, then washes his hands and dries them.

'Can I come in yet?'

'God. Can't I even go to the toilet in peace?' He opens the door. Eva trots in. She stands on tiptoe, trying to peer into the toilet bowl, but isn't tall enough.

'What's it like, going to the toilet?'

'Oh, don't put your hands on there: we're about to eat lunch! Come here.' He picks her up and dips her hands under the running tap. She's exhausting.

'Ooh, it's like a big Jacuzzi,' she says, looking at the basin. He holds her next to the towel before setting her down.

'Right, straight through to the lounge. No stopping.'

Whilst they are sitting there side by side, eating their lunch, him offering her titbits – she tries nibbling at a slice of cucumber – the windows start to patter with rain. As if on cue, there's a bump at the back door – the cat flap. Once again, Eva jumps onto Mr Lewis, her eyes wide in fright. 'Don't worry, she can't get in on her own. But I need to let her in, poor thing. Another reason you need to go back upstairs.' Eva pulls a face.

'Poor thing?' she says, as the cat appears at the patio doors, mewling and peering in.

'Come on, playtime's over,' he says. Eva reluctantly climbs into his hand.

Mr Lewis takes her upstairs and pops her down on the bedroom floor. She saunters over to the bed, dragging her feet. 'Oh, come on. Don't make me feel guilty. We've had fun, haven't we? You don't have to go back to sleep yet. You can mess about in here for a while.'

'And do what?'

'I don't know. Watch Lottie's telly. I don't know what dolls do. Play with your friends, Bimbo and, what's her boyfriend called?'

Eva scoffs. 'He's as plastic as she is. I don't think he likes women anyway – if you know what I mean.' This makes Mr Lewis chuckle.

'Well, what about soldier boy here?' He picks up an action figure, a hand-me-down from one of Lottie's cousins. 'Surely he's more your type – rugged, full of muscles.'

'Ugh. No thanks. He's plastic too; even his pants are plastic. He's not big like you anyway.'

'Stop saying how big I am! I'm not big, I'm just normal. I'm big to you because you're a doll.'

'Well, whatever. I can't talk to them, can I? I think I'll try on some clothes instead. Will you put the telly on for me, Mr Lewis?' He sighs. 'The music channels.' He does as she says and turns the sound down. 'Can you put the remote on the floor please?' She kicks off her shoes, then presses the channel button with a tiny foot till she gets to Vintage TV. Madonna's 'Material Girl' video is on. Eva navigates her foot to the volume button.

'Not too loud,' he says. 'Right. I'll leave you to it. Just keep the noise down. Bye, Eva. Until next time.' Eva looks sad.

'Bye, Mr Lewis.' He leaves, shutting the door behind him.

Mr Lewis lets the disgruntled cat in through the patio doors. She rubs her wet fur against his legs, purring. Then she goes straight to the spot on the sofa where Eva had been and has a sniff. Apart from the music and a few bumps from upstairs, which Stella also hears, Mr Lewis manages to get about an hour of relative peace and quiet.

This is interrupted by drumming on the bedroom door. The cat pays attention. Then the drumming is followed by a faint voice. 'Mr Lewis!' It couldn't last, he thinks. The banging gets louder, the shouting too. He gets up from his chair and stands at the bottom of the stairs. 'Mr Lewis! Come quick! I think I need the toilet!' Oh no. Does she genuinely mean this or is it just an attention thing? What if she *does* need to go? Where would she do it? How would she do it?

More pummelling. 'Mr Lewis, I think I need a pee!' She sounds panic-stricken. And well she might. To her it must feel like when a girl gets her first period, he thinks – a foreign sensation, terrifying, not knowing what it is or how to deal with it. This brings to the fore another dreadful prospect for Mr Lewis. What if she starts menstruating? How will he deal with that? He isn't equipped. These are female matters. Where will this end? What's he started here? You haven't started anything, he tells himself; you didn't make her wake up. With these thoughts racing through his brain, he dashes up the stairs.

He's just about to push open the bedroom door, saying 'Eva, get away from the door,' when he notices the cat has followed him up.

'Mr Lewis, I'm going to wet myself!'

'Oh God. No, Stella, get away!' He pushes the cat with his foot.

'Don't let that beast in here!' Eva cries. He hears the patter of her feet running away. It's no good. Stella can hear her. Mr Lewis picks the cat up and takes her into his and Mrs Lewis's bedroom, chucking her onto the bed. He closes the door and marches back to Lottie's room.

'Eva, I'm coming in!'

'No. Don't come in, it's too late. Just wait!' Mr Lewis stands at the door, his heart pounding, his mind boggling.

'Eva?' He knocks on the door.

Eva: A grown-up fairy tale

'Wait!' He can hear Stella scratching and pawing at his bedroom door. Jesus Christ. He's at his wits' end. 'OK. You can come in now.'

Mr Lewis walks in. A rather shamefaced Eva is sitting on the floor at the base of a bedpost. 'I had to go,' she says.

'Where?' He searches the floor, which is strewn with tiny clothes, for any signs of damp. How will he explain it? Blame the cat? Eva points to a toy saucepan with a lid on it.

'Oh,' he says.

'What's happening to me, Mr Lewis?'

'It must have been all that water.'

'I'm just glad I was wearing a skirt. I nearly didn't make it.' He notices her outfit for the first time. She's wearing a pink rah-rah skirt and a vest top, presumably borrowed from Bimbo. Her hair is done up in a ponytail. It's strange seeing her in something different, especially with her arms and shoulders on display. She sees him looking. 'Do you like it?' she says, standing up. 'Look, I even found some pants.'

'No! Don't do that!' he says, but it's too late. She's already hoisted up her skirt to show him. She's got no shame. Mr Lewis blushes.

'Don't worry, they're clean. It's not like Bimbo ever does anything in them. Erm, that reminds me, would you mind getting rid of the ... you know, the pan, please. And don't look at it – just chuck it down the toilet.' How has his life come to this? What is he? A bedside nurse now? He sighs and picks up the tiny saucepan, keeping his finger firmly on the lid. She follows him across the room. 'Where's that horrible beast?'

'She's locked in the bedroom. Why?'

'Oh. Can I have a bath then, please? I feel kind of dirty now.'

'No, Eva, you can't! Look, this has got to stop. The day's over. Don't keep pushing it. I'm dumping this and then you're going back to sleep. We've had more than enough excitement for one day. I don't need any more incidents ... or accidents.'

'But I don't want to go back to sleep yet.'

'Tough. I'm walking out of the house, so you haven't got a choice. Just stay in here whilst I do this. And get all this mess back in the box.' He closes the door on her. He chucks the pale liquid into the toilet bowl, wrinkling his nose. There's barely a thimble full. From across the corridor he can hear Stella miaowing to get out. He rinses the pan out and dries it with tissue paper. After flushing the toilet, he returns to the bedroom. He knocks on the door. 'Eva, I'm coming in. Mind out of the way.' Eva's sulking on Lottie's pillow. Mr Lewis ignores her and turns the telly off. 'Right, you've got five minutes to get changed and get back into position – in your trouser suit – and lose the pants, too. Then I'm walking out. Sorry. That's final. I'll come and check on you, so no monkey business.' She ignores him, her arms folded across her chest, pouting, staring straight ahead. He leaves her to it.

Mr Lewis opens his bedroom door to let the cat out. Nuzzling her way out into the corridor with a whine, she brushes against his legs. Then she heads straight to Lottie's bedroom door and looks at him, letting out another cry. This could be a problem. 'Come on, Stella,' he says, heading downstairs. The cat lingers. 'Come on!'

He ushers her downstairs with a sweep of his arm. She runs down ahead of him, tail up.

Passing time for a bit before leaving the house, Mr Lewis checks for messages and missed calls on his phone. There aren't any. He puts the kettle on, then does a sweep of the lounge and kitchen, collecting up recycling stuff for the bin – newspapers, old TV guides, empty tins, wine bottles and cereal packets. 'Right, that should do it,' he says to himself. He opens a patio door and steps outside to the recycling bin, then chucks everything in it before heading back inside. After washing his hands, he pours water into his mug. Better go and check. She'd better be in position.

Getting weary of it, he heads back upstairs. He opens Lottie's bedroom door and peers round it. Eva is in exactly the same place, turned back into a doll – and, save for some shoes, without a stitch on. Typical. 'You little so and so,' he says. 'I know you can hear me, Eva.' It seems strange that this is possible when she's in a lifeless state. 'And I know what you're up to. You want me to move you so you come alive again. Well, it's not going to work.'

He walks over to the bed. She's supine, arms and legs straight, eyes wide, staring at the ceiling. It's the first time he's seen her like this – without clothes on as a doll; he's grateful it does nothing for him. But it crosses his mind that if he touches her now she'll come alive, naked. Perhaps that's part of her plan. She seems hell bent on it. 'Where are your clothes?' he says, yanking down the bed cover. They aren't there. 'What have you done with them?' He lifts up the pillow. Nothing. It's as if she's hidden them on purpose. 'Shit!' He feels like shaking her. But then she'd have won. He's sick of her running rings round him. 'You know what? I don't care. You can stay there until Dianne gets back. And then as soon as I get a chance, with her in the house, you're going back in the box, to the bottom – with or without clothes!' He covers her up with the duvet, and after one last futile look under the bed for the clothes leaves the room.

CHAPTER 6

When Mr Lewis hears his wife's car pull up, a little later than usual, he feels a mixture of emotions. One, relief that normal, rational life is being resumed. Two, a little nervous anxiety that Eva is still in the bed. Three, guilt: it's starting to feel as if he's actually having an affair, which he doesn't like. He loves his wife. OK, things aren't as physical as they were before they had Lottie, but they still have their moments; they still try.

'Hi. How's your day been?' Mrs Lewis asks as she enters the lounge, clutching some shopping bags.

'Are there any more?' Mr Lewis asks, getting up.

'No, this is it. Just some bits for dinner.' She pushes the door closed with her foot. He takes the bags from her and kisses her on the cheek. She smells of perfume, hairspray and cooking. 'Have you been busy?' An insane voice in his head makes him want to laugh hysterically, drop the carrier bags he's holding and fall at her feet, saying, 'I've been changing a living doll's bedpan!' He ignores it and takes the bags into the kitchen.

'Oh, you know. The usual. Nothing much to report.' Mrs Lewis's face is a picture of disappointment and apprehension as she picks up the mail from the coffee table. There's never any good post these days. She puts it back down; nothing worth opening. She follows her husband into the kitchen.

'Is lasagne all right for dinner?' she says, yawning and running her hands through her hair.

'Yes, fine. Madam will complain, I suppose.'

'Well, tough. She always moans, but she eats it. Right, I'm going upstairs; I need a shower. I feel gross. It was fish and chip day.'

Mr Lewis's ears prick up. This could be just the opportunity he needs to get Eva dressed and back in the box. 'Yes, you do smell a bit funky,' he teases.

'Does that mean you don't want to join me?' Mr Lewis laughs awkwardly. It's a while since she's said anything like that. It's a while since they've *done* anything like that. Is she joking or does she mean it? He doesn't know what to say. 'I'll take that as a no, then.' Mrs Lewis heads upstairs, leaving him standing there.

He begins to put the shopping away – noisily banging cupboards; trying to sound busy. Then there's a shout from upstairs. 'What the hell's been going on in here?' Mr Lewis freezes. 'There's muddy cat prints all over the bed ... and on the door!'

'Er, Stella brought in a mouse again – half alive. It was a nightmare. I had to shut her in our room whilst I got rid of it!'

'Well, you could have shut her outside. I'm going to have to strip the bed now.' Shit, the cat flap, thinks Mr Lewis. Thank God she reminded him. He goes to unlock it, then saunters upstairs to see the extent of the mess. His wife is stripping the bed.

'Yes, sorry about that,' he says, inspecting the door. 'It was raining, you see. She was wet when she came in. That's why I couldn't put her outside. I'll get a sponge from the bathroom.' He wipes down the door and helps Mrs Lewis strip the pillows.

'I might as well do Lottie's while I'm at it. It hasn't been washed for a while – probably stinks.'

'No! I'll do it. You go and have a shower. It's my fault. I'll stick them all in the machine.'

'Are you sure? Haven't you got work to do?'

'No. Not at the minute.'

'No movement on the Simon residence I take it, then?' This has become a bit of an obsession for both of them.

'No, not over the weekend. I might apply a bit of pressure this week. Try and hurry things along. You have to be careful how much you push.'

'Yes, I know. It's been dragging on for so long, though.'

Mr Lewis takes their bedsheets downstairs, then waits for the sound of the shower before going into Lottie's room. He's got to work quickly. First, where are those damn clothes? He's got to find them. Whipping the duvet off the bed, he inadvertently sends Eva spinning onto the floor on her front. Then he pulls the cover off the duvet, but there's nothing inside it. With no time for sentiment, he chucks both duvet and cover on top of Eva before stripping the sheet off the bed. This is chucked on the pile too. Then he makes a start on the pillow cases. The clothes aren't in them either. After a quick check under the mattress, he drops to his knees and looks under the bed again. But further this time: pulling out boxes and pushing them aside.

There, right at the back and in the dark and dust, are the crumpled up clothes. Both sets. 'You little minx,' he says, getting on his stomach to crawl under the bed. He has to stretch. She must have shoved them down the other side of the bed, near the wall. He pulls them out. The trousers of the suit are inside out. 'Oh, for Christ's sake.' He tries in vain to turn them back, but it's impossible. 'Forget it. What am I doing?' he says, losing patience.

Grabbing Eva from under the bedclothes, he begins to dress her. First, he has to remove her shoes. He's sweating now. How can such a little thing cause so much trouble? She looks so innocent when she's asleep, as if butter wouldn't melt. He puts on the jacket, trying to pop the buttons with his big, clumsy fingers, trying to ignore the fact that they keep nudging her hard plastic boobs. Same with the trousers, tugging them on roughly, still inside out. 'I'm not happy with you, you know, not happy at all,' he says, holding her out in front of him in his fist. She stares blankly back at him, her hair tied back. 'Shit!' the ponytail. He yanks out the little band she's put in it. 'Right. You're done. You're going in the box.' He refrains from saying 'never again' this time as he chucks her in. The spare set of clothes is tossed in too, along with the shoes. Then he feels guilty and stands Eva upright.

Grabbing the washing, he heads out onto the landing. Mrs Lewis shouts from the bedroom, 'Did someone call?' When did she come out of the shower?

'No.'

'Oh. I thought I heard you talking to someone.'

Shit. Mr Lewis bends to pick up the other bedding. 'Just talking to myself, dear – first sign of madness and all that!'

* * * * * * * *

Later that evening, Mr Lewis has one last little obstacle to overcome.

Mrs Lewis is washing up after dinner, as Mr Lewis reads with Lottie on the sofa. 'Where's this little cup come from?' Mrs Lewis calls.

'What's that?'

She walks into the lounge, holding a tiny turquoise cup in her pink, rubber-gloved hands (she does enough washing up at work; it's ruining her hands). 'Have you been entertaining pixies for lunch again?' She places the little cup on the coffee table, covered in soapsuds as if frothing with beer.

'That's from my dolls' teaset,' says Lottie.

'Well what's it doing on the kitchen windowsill?'

'I found it on the floor,' Mr Lewis pipes up. 'I nearly hoovered it up.'

'What, you've hoovered today?'

'Yes, just a quick whip-round.'

'Well, you didn't do a very good job!'

'I'm a bloke, aren't I? Blokes aren't meant to be good at housework. Are they, sweetheart?' He tickles his daughter in the ribs, making her giggle.

'Don't listen to your father, he's being sexist.'

'What's sexist?'

'It means he's an idiot.'

Conversation over; another potential minefield

averted. But Mr Lewis hates the lying; how does it come so easily?

Once Lottie has been tucked in, a similar scene to the previous Monday develops; the stresses and anxieties of the day are giving way to alcohol-induced contemplation. Mr Lewis is lulled by a couple of bottles of beer, and little things from the day keep coming back to him – the jokes and games he and Eva share, the silly things she comes out with…

'What are you smiling at?'

'Oh, nothing. Just something Ian sent me earlier.' Ian was Mr Lewis's closest friend.

'Oh. More sexist jokes? That reminds me: don't forget we've got the barbecue coming up. You'll have to pull it out of the shed and clean it up.'

Every year the family hold a spring bank holiday barbecue. What started as a one-off has become a bit of a tradition; a herald to the start of the summer. A small gathering of close family and friends: a few neighbours, Mrs Lewis's sister and kids, Mr Lewis's brother, Paul, and his wife and kids, and best buddy Ian and his latest squeeze. And not forgetting, of course, his work partner David and his perma-tanned wife. No doubt David will turn up in his latest sports car, bragging about how much work he's got on and the holiday they've just got back from. Going into business with friends always seems like such a good idea, but rarely is – their relationship is becoming ever more distant and strained.

'It's not this Monday, is it?'

'No, a week on Monday, the 25th.' Mr Lewis breathes a mental sigh of relief. Funny, he usually looks forward to the annual barbecue, he likes to socialise;

but this year he can't be bothered with it. He'd rather be on his own, just him and Eva; Monday's their day now. God, what's he thinking? What's coming over him? 'Are you OK?' Mrs Lewis says.

'Yes, just thinking it would be nice if we could get this deal tied up by then. You know, some good news, something to celebrate. Not much chance of that, though.'

'Well, you never know. Things can change quickly.'

****

Things don't change quickly, not that week anyway. The Simons do, however, finally agree to lower their asking price by £3,000. A considerable amount of asbestos was discovered in one of the property's bathrooms during the initial survey; it's riddled with the stuff and needs ripping out – a matter that Gaunt wants the sellers to deal with rather than him. David did the survey, and Mr Lewis knew straightaway it was going to be a problem. In his desperation for the sale, he'd briefly considered asking his partner not to disclose it. But this would have been unethical beyond belief, and would probably have come back to bite him. So in the end he decided not to. He is glad about this now: it would have given him sleepless nights.

Lowering the asking price is something Mr Lewis suggested. It's taken the Simons a long time to come round to it. Hopefully this is the last stumbling block. Now all that is needed is Gaunt to agree to it. Mr Lewis passes on the news of this latest compromise. Gaunt reacts non-committally with one of his usual cryptic expressions – something about 'getting all his ducks in a row'.

Mr Lewis is trying his best to concentrate on work, but by mid-week something peculiar is happening to him; something he can no longer deny. There are no two ways about it; he can't wait till the next Monday comes around, and the urge to wake Eva is becoming harder and harder to resist.

Somehow he manages to get through the week, telling himself it'll make Monday more special. And as the weekend rolls around, the happier he feels. He feels a lightness of being, a boyish energy that he hasn't felt in years – not since his uni days; not since he met his wife. It's something he can't quite put his finger on. He listens to music more – in his car, pottering about at home; always the '80s station. Lyrics take on new meanings – hidden messages in almost every song; he wonders if Eva can hear them too. He drinks more, he dreams more. He puts everything down to the end in sight to the Simon–Gaunt deal.

On Sunday evening, Mr Lewis comes back down to earth with a bump. Lottie is ill; throwing up and with a temperature. Despite his fatherly concern for his daughter, he can't help wondering how this will affect him. What if she's too ill to go to school? As they put Lottie to bed, he says to her, 'See how you feel in the morning; you just need a good night's sleep.'

'Oh, she won't be going to school tomorrow. They're not allowed back for forty-eight hours if they've been sick,' his wife says. Mr Lewis's heart sinks.

'But what if she's OK in the morning? It's not like the school knows she's been sick.'

'That's not the point. *We'll* know she's been sick. It's not fair on the other kids. I wouldn't want Lottie catching something from someone else. It's not like it matters, anyway: you're off work on Mondays.'

'I'm not "off work" – I'm working at home. I've still got stuff to do.'

'Well, she won't bother you.'

'But what if I have to go on a viewing?'

'I don't know! Chantelle or Owen will have to deal with it. That's what you pay them for.'

'But what if Gaunt turns up? You know what he's like.'

'He'll just have to bloody wait till two o'clock, won't he? I'll be back by then.'

There are no further incidents in the night, and predictably Lottie seems as right as rain in the morning, prompting Mr Lewis to try one last time. 'Look, there's nothing wrong with her. Do you feel well enough to go to school, honey?'

'She's not going! It doesn't matter how she feels.'

'But I want to go, Mummy.'

'No, you're not going, and that's final. Rules are there for a reason. You don't have to work in a school, Stephen, so you don't know what it's like. What if Lottie tells someone by accident she's been sick? How will that make me look? I work in the kitchen, for Christ's sake.'

They both wave Mrs Lewis off for work, both of them unhappy – an understatement in Mr Lewis's case. Nobody likes having something taken away from them, something they've been looking forward to; it makes them feel put out, hard done by. He wishes he'd woken Eva up in the week now. It seems an age away till the next Monday. But then it dawns on him that the next Monday is the bank holiday – the barbecue. This sends him into a further spiral of misery. He feels resentment towards his daughter for being at home with him. But he hates himself for this, and forces himself to snap out of it.

'Right, what do you want to do? Daddy's got to work.'

'I'll just watch telly for a bit.'

'OK, just not too loud.' This sounds familiar. Mr Lewis switches on the computer, but no part of his brain is thinking of work. He feels as if he ought to go and explain to Eva what's going on. Surely she'll be wondering why he hasn't woken her up. Or perhaps she doesn't know when it's Monday. No, of course she does; she's not stupid. She would have heard the conversation in Lottie's room – sometimes he forgets this. He looks across at his daughter, watching cartoons, bless her, and decides to slip upstairs.

'Where are you going, Daddy?'

'Oh, I'm just going to the toilet, honey.' He goes through the motions of pretending to go to the bathroom, and then, checking that Lottie is still watching telly, slips across the landing to her room. He heads straight for the toy box. Eva is further down the box than he left her, her trousers still inside out. Carefully, Mr Lewis extricates her. 'Eva,' he whispers. 'It's me.' What a stupid thing to say. He's holding her too close to his mouth as well, as if she's a microphone. He hopes his breath doesn't smell. He holds her further away, facing towards him. 'I'm sorry. Lottie's downstairs. She's off school today, so I can't wake you up. There's nothing I can do. I'm annoyed about it too. I'll wake you up again as soon as I can, I promise. I'm really sorry.' He lays her gently back in the box, facing upwards – just another toy amongst many others; her perennially cheerful expression belying what she must be going through. He can't imagine how frustrating it must be.

Then an idea comes to him. Why doesn't he take the box downstairs? That way, at least she'll get some stimulation – a break from the monotony. Without further thought, he picks up the box and carries it downstairs. 'I've brought you some toys to play with,' he says, putting the box down near Lottie.

'Oh, that's OK. I'm watching telly.'

'But it'll be nice to play for a bit. Look, you've got – what's her name?' He pulls Eva out and holds her up.

'Eva,' Lottie says, with barely a glance.

'Eva. You've got Bim... this one...' He starts lining them up, sitting them on the sofa next to Lottie so Eva can watch telly. He feels a twinge of guilt at this, manipulating his daughter in this way, but tells himself he's doing it for Eva's benefit. 'You've got her silly boyfriend. What's his name?'

'He's not her boyfriend, Daddy, he's just her friend.'

'Oh, I thought he was. Doesn't he like girls?' A little joke, also for Eva's benefit.

'Yes. He *was*, but Eva stole him from her.'

'Oh right.' This really *was* getting interesting.

'And how did she feel about having her boyfriend stolen?'

'She was cross. She cried. They don't like each other now.'

'Oh, right.'

'Sometimes Eva steals her clothes too, so they fight with each other.' Lottie picks both the dolls up and starts tussling with them to demonstrate. This is getting a bit strange, Mr Lewis thinks.

'Well, I've got an idea. Why doesn't Eva give this one her clothes back?' He plucks Bimbo off Lottie and wiggles her about. 'And then Eva can get her own dress back. Perhaps then she'll hand the boyfriend back too – and then they can be friends again.' It would make his life a damn sight easier if Eva wore her own dress instead of wanting to get changed all the time.

'That's a good idea, Daddy. Can I have a drink of squash, please?'

'Sure.' As he walks into the kitchen, out of the corner of his eye he can see Lottie swapping the doll's clothes. At least that's something that's come out of today, he thinks. When he returns, Eva is back in her dress and Lottie is dressing Bimbo. He puts the drink on the coffee table. 'I think she looks pretty in that dress; it suits her.'

'Yes, me too.'

Mr Lewis goes back to his work and Lottie soon tires of playing with the dolls. 'Can I play on the tablet, Daddy?'

'You can if it's charged. Otherwise you'll have to plug it in. Have you finished watching telly? You can't do both.'

'Yes.' Mr Lewis is about to switch the telly off when he thinks of Eva. Instead, he turns over to the music channels – trying to keep everyone happy.

Soon it's lunchtime, and Mr Lewis and his daughter sit side by side on the sofa to eat, just as he and Eva did. He feels guilty about this too and decides to put the box back first; it's making him feel uncomfortable knowing she's watching. 'Have you finished with these?' he says, putting the dolls back in the box.

'Yes, Daddy.'

He takes the box upstairs. Alone with Eva in Lottie's room, he says, 'Well, at least you got your dress back.'

CHAPTER 7

By Wednesday evening Mr Lewis is pining for Eva, for her company. He longs to feel the give of her body as it softens in his hand, to hear her waterfall laughter. His stomach jolts whenever Lottie says: 'Oh, can I come?' in response to his wife's announcements that she's nipping to the shops. But still he daren't risk it, not for ten minutes or so. As adorable as Eva is, she's a magnet for trouble and mischief – a sprite; poison lips, treacle tongue. He needs more time. Swimming club it is then, he decides. He looks forward to it all day. He feels nervous as he says goodbye to them. How will she react? Will she be cross with him again? With no time to lose he dashes upstairs.

His heart is romping in his chest as he picks her up, adrenaline pumping through his veins. 'Eva, Eva, wake up!' To his relief, she comes to life straight away; no games today. She immediately launches herself at his face and neck, planting a kiss firmly on his lips. It hurts a little, like a mini head butt. She grabs at his shirt collar for grip and he has to catch her to stop her from falling. 'Easy, easy!' he says, laughing and turning red.

'You love me, Mr Lewis. You do, you do, you do. I can see it in your face! You said I was pretty!' She tries to kiss him again, but he stops her, putting his hand up.

'Stop it, Eva, you're being silly.' He pulls her away and places her on the bed.

'You have missed me, though, haven't you, Mr Lewis, as much as I've missed you?'

'Perhaps a little.'

'Oh, it's been horrible. Last Monday was the worst day of my life. I wanted to cry and cry and cry. I *was* crying inside.'

'I know. There's something I need to tell you, actually, whilst we've got the chance.'

'What? You're leaving Mrs Lewis and you're going to run away with me?'

'Er, no. I'm afraid not. It's about next Monday.' He looks grave. Eva's little face drops.

'Oh no. Don't tell me Lottie's going to be at home again. Please. I won't be able to take it.'

'Not just Lottie. Mrs Lewis too *and* other people. It's a bank holiday, you see: we're having a barbecue.'

Eva puts her face in her hands, her shoulders slumped. 'What's a barbecue?' she says, her voice flat.

'It's a kind of party, where you cook outside for people.'

'And I'll be stuck in here. I wish I could go to a party. I wish I could go outside.' She begins to sob into her hands. It breaks his heart. Mr Lewis strokes her hair with his thumb.

'You will, I promise. We've just got to wait. One more week and things will get back to normal. I'll take you outside then.'

'But that's ages away,' she says, looking up, her big eyes wet with tears.

'It's not. Not really. Look, we've got now. We've got nearly an hour. What do you want to do? Anything you like.'

'I want to go outside.'

'Anything but go outside. It's too risky; we haven't got time.'

'Have a bath then. In the sink downstairs.'

'Downstairs? Are you mad? That's not spending time together anyway.'

'It is if *you* bath me.' She bites her lip.

'I don't think so, Eva. It wouldn't be right.'

'Why not?'

'Just because. What do you want a bath for anyway?'

'I'm starting to smell funny.' She lifts her arms up and sniffs her armpits to demonstrate.

'I doubt that.' Mr Lewis considers for a moment. 'I suppose I *could* run a bath for you; not too much trouble can come of it. But only a shallow one, mind, and you'll have to be quick. No more than ten minutes. No messing about. And it'll have to be the bathroom. It's less risky. Come on.' He picks her up.

Mr Lewis pushes open the bathroom door. He removes the toothbrush cup from its metal holder on the wall and places it on the windowsill. Drying the little round soap well beneath it, he sits Eva in it next to the cold tap. Her feet are bare. They dangle over the edge of the basin.

Eva: A grown-up fairy tale

Mr Lewis turns on the hot tap till it runs warm. It begins to steam. Eva leans away. 'Not too hot, Mr Lewis. I'll burn!' He turns the tap down to a trickle, then pulls up the metal rod between the taps so that the plug nestles in the basin, which begins to fill. Eva watches, fascinated.

'Mind out,' he says, as he turns on the cold tap, which juts out near her head. He swirls the water round with his hand, checking the temperature. Satisfied at the level, about three inches deep in the middle, he turns off the tap.

'Is it ready, Mr Lewis?'

'Not quite. We might as well do this properly.' He grabs some of Lottie's bubblebath, a pink one, and pours a few drops in. He mixes it in. The water clouds slightly then turns into foamy bubbles. Eva claps her hands together in glee and stands up. 'Can I go in now?' She begins to reach for the buttons at the back of her dress.

'Wait!' says Mr Lewis. 'Not yet. Wait till I've left the room. First, though, a few rules. Have you ever had a bath before?'

'Not a proper one. Only with Lottie whilst I was, you know, before I was…'

'Well, you know not to put your head under for too long, right? Because you'll drown.'

'What's drown?'

'It means you won't be able to breathe and you'll die.' He's starting to regret this. He hasn't really thought it through. 'In fact, don't put your head under at all, and don't swallow the water. It's not a drink.'

'Yes, I know that, Mr Lewis. It's got bubbles in it.'

'And when you're ready to get out – and this is important – drain the basin first and then dry yourself. Don't sit or stand on the edge. It's a long way down and it could be slippy.' Eva looks over the edge and sits down quickly. 'Here's a towel.' He places a dry flannel next to the hot tap. Hang your dress on the cup holder here, and make sure you're fully dressed before you call me back in.'

'But how do I drain the basin?'

'You push down on top of this rod.' He presses it with his finger to demonstrate. The basin sucks and gurgles, making Eva jump. He quickly pulls it up again. 'You see?'

'Yes, Mr Lewis.'

'Right. Enjoy your bath. You've got ten minutes. I'll call you when it's time.'

'Are you sure you don't want to stay?' she asks coquettishly.

'Quite sure.' Mr Lewis leaves the bathroom and closes the door. Once outside, he starts to wonder if he's doing the right thing. He's taking a big risk. What if Dianne and Lottie come back suddenly for some reason? Or what if something happens to Eva? An accident? Checking his watch, he goes downstairs. He tries to watch telly, but feels on edge and can't concentrate. He paces around, glancing out of the dining room window in case Dianne's car pulls up.

Before long, ten minutes is up. He daren't leave it any longer; Eva needs to get dry. He climbs the stairs to the landing and listens outside the door. From inside the bathroom he can hear the sound of splashing and Eva singing to herself – 'Material Girl' by Madonna.

Eva: A grown-up fairy tale

It makes him smile. 'Eva. Your ten minutes is up. You need to come out.'

'What, already? That was quick. Do I have to?'

'Yes. No monkey business, remember? Just drain the basin, get yourself dried and then call me when you're dressed. I'll be across the landing. And be careful!'

'Oh, all right,' Eva groans. Mr Lewis enters the bedroom and stares out of the window, feeling anxious.

Shortly, Eva calls him. 'Mr Lewis, I'm ready!'

Mr Lewis returns to the bathroom. 'I hope you're decent. I'm coming in!' he says. Before waiting for an answer, he pushes open the door. To his shock, he's met with the sight of Eva reclining in her bath, Cleopatra-like, hands behind her head. She's smiling. Her hair is wet and her cheeks are flushed. The shiny little mounds of her breasts are half-exposed; her tiny nipples, watermelon-pink, bobbing on the surface of the water. But that's not all; because of his height, he has an aerial view into the basin. Amongst the miniature islands of foam bubbles and milky, semi-opaque water there's a little black triangle between her legs, exactly the same colour as her hair. It makes him feel strange. 'Eva!' he says, shielding his eyes, his face crimson. He reaches for the plug-rod and bangs it down with his palm. 'What a nasty trick. I told you to call me when you were dressed!'

'Sorry, Mr Lewis, I couldn't get the rod to go down.' Mr Lewis turns around to face the wall. He hears the shallow water gurgle away and Eva's body squeaking in the empty basin as she stands up. Mr Lewis is confronted by his alarmed countenance in the mirror. He can't look at himself and averts his eyes. To his horror, and pleasure, in a bottom corner of the mirror he can just see a reflection of Eva's head and slender shoulder. Unable to help himself, he leans forward, adjusting himself slightly so he can see more. He sees a white flannel, parted like a robe, to reveal pink skin within and a flash of that matted black velvet triangle. He slams the cabinet door shut so that he can't see any more.

Once she's dressed and dried, but still flushed pink, he carries Eva into Lottie's bedroom so that she can brush her hair. She uses one of Bimbo's little brushes. 'Smell my hair, Mr Lewis; it smells nice.'

'Hmm,' he says, giving it a sniff. He preferred it before, *au naturelle*. It smells too human now, as back to front as this sounds. 'It's still wet,' he says. 'That won't do. What if it doesn't dry in time?' She looks different with her wet hair scraped back. 'Come on, we'll have to dry it.' He carries her into his and Mrs Lewis's bedroom and pops her onto the bed.

As he plugs the hairdryer into the wall and presses the switch down, Eva says: 'I like it in here, Mr Lewis. I wish I could come in here more often. Mrs Lewis is so lucky.' She crawls to the top of the bed and pulls back the covers, as if to get in.

'No you don't,' he says, grabbing her leg and pulling her back. They both laugh as she struggles, kicking his hand. 'Right, sit on the edge of the bed and hold still.' He switches on the hairdryer. It's huge compared to Eva and as loud as a jet engine.

'Turn it off, it's too loud!' she screams. 'What if it hurts?'

'It won't!' He turns the setting to cool and, standing a foot or so away, aims the hairdryer at Eva's hair. The sudden blast takes her breath away and sends her flying flat onto her back. 'Sorry!' he says. He stands further back, two feet or so, and the waft of the hairdryer gently caresses her locks. She tenses with her fists clutching the duvet cover, eyes closed. When she gets used to the feeling she starts to enjoy it, and moves her face from side to side, offering her fine cheekbones to the wind like a dog with its head out of a car window.

'I feel like a movie star!' she cries. She looks like one as well, Mr Lewis thinks, continuing to caress her with the hairdryer. He surprises himself with his gentleness towards her, his willingness to indulge her. She stands up on the bed, legs astride, hands on hips. 'Do me from below, Mr Lewis – like Marilyn!' She'd seen the famous photo on the telly, and loved it. Again, Mr Lewis obliges her, blowing upwards with the hairdryer. Her dress balloons around her and she laughs that laugh of hers, pushing her dress back down demurely, but not before her knickers have been displayed to the world.

Mr Lewis turns the hairdryer off and it winds down, whirring to a halt as Eva's laughter dies. She plonks herself down, slightly out of breath. They both fall silent for a moment. Mr Lewis is contemplative, knowing that he really ought to turn her back to a doll; he has to go outside to do it, and also put the bathroom straight. It makes him feel sad. Every time she wakes up, it's a little adventure, a little bit of magic; there's always something happening. She paints his days with a kaleidoscope of vivid, swirling colours, when otherwise they are monochrome. 'Are you OK, Mr Lewis?'

'Come on,' he says. 'I need to change you back.'

****

That night Mr Lewis has some strange dreams. There's an '80s soundtrack and Eva is the star. She's in different music videos, dressed up and acting out the parts. 'Material Girl' by Madonna, dressed in a pink off-the-shoulder dress, necklace and white gloves. 'Mickey' by Toni Basil – doing her pom-pom routine in a cheerleader's outfit. 'Addicted to Love' by Robert Palmer, in a tight black top, heels and skirt, guitar in hand, singing into a microphone. 'If I Could Turn Back Time' by Cher, sitting astride a large toy cannon.

Next, he is replaying the scene when he entered the bathroom earlier. The bathroom is steamier than it was, but Eva is the same: the same flush to her cheeks, the same knowing look on her face, that inviting gap in her teeth as she opens her mouth to speak. But this time, instead of shielding his eyes, he keeps on looking. He brushes her damp hair off her forehead with his finger. His hand covers her; it is three times the width of her body. She takes his index finger and places it on her slippery chest, between her boobs. With both hands, she steers his finger below the surface of the water, down her body as she shivers, to that waiting shadow... He wakes up sweating.

CHAPTER 8

The day of the barbecue comes around. The day is hot. The lawns are mown, the edges have been strimmed. The radio is on – a top one hundred '80s bank holiday countdown; it couldn't be more perfect. Mr Lewis is drunk. He's starting to unravel a little: last Friday he called Chantelle Eva. Heaven forbid he should do that to his wife. There's something manic about him, manic-depressive almost. His earlier funk when he woke up this morning – the prospect of the barbecue at the expense of his Monday with Eva – has given way to behaviour bordering on hyperactivity. A combination of the clink of ice in tall glasses on a summer's day – one of the best sounds in the world – music, food, people, the smell of the lilac, the white of the rambling clematis, has whipped him into a frenzy.

He wants to tell his partner David what he really thinks of him *and* his 'tangerine' wife (as Eva would say). He feels horny, sexually frustrated. He can't stop looking at his best friend Ian's hot new gym-body girlfriend's breasts in that tight top. He wants to smack his wife's arse in front of everyone, to put his hand up her dress. He wants to pick his daughter up and spin her around. He wants to confess to Ian, in private, about Eva; he feels as if he'll go mad if he doesn't tell someone. This he considers whilst looking at himself in the downstairs toilet mirror. His face is coloured from the sun, making his teeth appear whiter. 'You handsome fella,' he says to himself. But what if Ian wants to borrow her? To share her? To share his *'precious'*? He studies his reflection again; his eyes are narrow, mean-looking. God, I'm turning into Sméagol now, he thinks.

Thinking of Eva makes him want to wake her up, to see that Strawberry Mivvi smile that brightens up his days, to put his hand up *her* skirt. He couldn't. Not now. Not with all these people around. Could he? He dries his hands. Just you watch me. He slips out of the toilet and past the open back door, where adults are drunkenly playing a giant Jenga game on the patio. He sneaks through the dining room and up the stairs, his heart beating like a drum, into Lottie's room.

There she is in the toy box, his raven-haired, pre-Raphaelite princess; bored out of her brain, no doubt. As he reaches to pick her up, he feels as if he's crossing a line – that he's taking a crazy chance – but he doesn't care. He wants to whisper sweet nothings to her whilst people are downstairs, oblivious. 'Eva, Eva, ballerina, wake up.' He anticipates the softening of her body, the blink of her long lashes. 'Wake up, my little princess; I know you can hear me.' She's obviously toying with him, delaying it on purpose, or perhaps she's mad at him for something. He tickles her tummy with his finger. 'Eva, wake up. You were right. I do love you!' Still nothing; that's funny. There's a sudden creak on the landing, right outside the door, then the unmistakable sound of footsteps tiptoeing down the stairs. '*Shit!*'

He throws Eva back in the box. Now he's torn it. Who was it? What did they hear? No wonder she didn't wake up. He thought he'd made sure everyone was outside. Or had he? He's drunk. 'Shit,' he says again. He needs to get out of here. Who could it have been? Why didn't they come in? It couldn't have been Dianne; she'd have been in like a shot. Maybe it was one of the kids; that wouldn't have been so bad.

He leaves the room, closing the door, and goes into the spare room opposite. Keeping behind the curtain, he looks out onto the back lawn to see who's there. Dianne's talking to David – or rather listening to him (probably bragging as usual). Mrs Tangerine is talking to Mr Lewis's brother, Paul. One of his neighbours, a man, is chatting up his sister-in-law by the looks of it, showing her one of his tattoos. It's like some modern day-time version of *A Midsummer Night's Dream* out there, or a swinger's party where everyone appears to have swapped partners.

The only person he can see who hasn't is Ian; he's talking to another couple of neighbours, his arm around his girlfriend's back, his hand in her jeans back pocket. Most of the kids appear to be there too. Lottie is playing Swingball with her cousins. Mr Lewis climbs onto the bed to try and see down onto the patio, where he can hear laughter, but it's no use. Who's down there? Who's missing? There's a cheer as the Jenga crashes down.

Everyone on the lawn looks over and he darts back behind the curtain.

He looks out again, and as he does so he sees his other sister-in-law – Paul's wife, Hayley – step up onto the lawn to join his brother. Mr Lewis freezes. Where's *she* come from? The house or the patio? In her hand is a baby monitor – one of those little plastic walkie-talkies. It must have been her. She looks serious, tired as usual; two young children, one a baby. She puts her hair behind her ear and says something to Paul, who tilts his head to listen. He looks serious too. What the hell is she saying? Mr Lewis sees Paul glance up at the house, and he darts behind the curtain again. What's he doing, hiding in here? He's got to go and face the music, but he feels drained, rooted to the spot, no energy. He forces himself to go downstairs.

Outside, Hayley is talking to Dianne now, with her back to him. This isn't a good sign – especially as Dianne heard him talking to Eva the other day. There are a few kids on the patio, putting the Jenga back together, but no longer any adults. His mouth feels dry. He needs a drink. 'Here he is!' Paul says, still stuck with Mrs Tangerine. 'Where have you been hiding? And where's your drink?' Mr Lewis forces a smile. At least Paul's acting normally. 'Come and join us.' He probably wants to be saved from Mrs Tangerine.

'I'll just grab a beer,' Mr Lewis says. He goes over to the beer bucket, full of melting ice and water.

'*Daddy!*' Lottie cries, throwing herself at her father's legs. He scoops her up with one arm.

'Hi, sweetheart, are you being good?' She makes him feel normal. Mrs Lewis and Hayley turn around. His wife smiles, but Hayley doesn't; she looks him up and down. Mr Lewis looks away. He opens a beer, puts his daughter back down and goes to join Paul.

'So, how's the market?' his brother asks. 'Things picking up?'

Mr Lewis tries to engage in the conversation, but is more interested in what Hayley and Dianne are talking about. Anyway, he can't discuss just how quiet things are in front of his partner's wife. He distinctly hears Dianne say, 'Has she gone off?'

'Sounds like it,' Hayley replies, holding the monitor to her ear.

'Where's Zoe?' Mr Lewis asks Paul.

'Oh, upstairs in your room. Hope you don't mind. She's having a nap. She was getting grouchy.' This confirms it. It must have been Hayley. What did she hear? She was right outside the door. How long was she there?

The barbecue winds down without further incident, or the answers to these questions being revealed. On leaving, however, Hayley is noticeably awkward around Mr Lewis, unable to look him in the eye and evading the usual hug or kiss goodbye, using the shield of their baby and its considerable paraphernalia. Apart from this the party has been a success, with most people leaving in high spirits – and in some cases suitably inebriated. Mr Lewis continues to drink late into the evening.

Lottie is put to bed earlier than usual, and shortly afterwards the Lewises also retire. Mr Lewis is still feeling amorous; that feeling from earlier in the day hasn't gone away. And after they are satisfied their daughter is sound asleep, he and Mrs Lewis make love.

It's the first time in a while, and initially Mrs Lewis is surprised at her husband's unexpected interest. As she warms to the idea, her enthusiasm soon matches his – just at the point when his begins to wane, the alcohol taking its toll.

In the dark, and drunk, his mind starts to wander. Unable to help himself, Mr Lewis conjures up images of Eva, her dress blowing upwards, Marilyn-style, the flash of her pants, the dreams he had about her, the music videos. His body responds to the imagery, and spurred on by this he goes even further; he can't stop himself. He pictures Eva in the bath, her come-hither eyes, the reflection of her drying herself in the cabinet mirror, her voice: 'Sorry, Mr Lewis, I couldn't get the rod to go down.' This tips him over the edge and a sudden spasm grips him. He goes to pull out, as is the norm, but to his surprise his wife cries '*No!*' and grips him to her, refusing to let him go at so crucial a moment. They climax together for the first time in years – not since they last tried for a baby. It feels so wrong, yet so right, so irresponsible, yet such a relief.

Afterwards he rolls off onto his back, both of them breathing hard. Mrs Lewis shifts and drapes herself across him. 'Whoops,' she says into his chest. Mr Lewis barely hears her. He's staring at the ceiling in the dark, eyes wide, alarmed and disgusted at himself. *What's happening to me?* he thinks.

CHAPTER 9

The next morning Mr Lewis has a hangover – on a work day too, which exacerbates his depression. He's ashamed and regretful about the previous night, in every respect. What was he thinking? What was Dianne thinking? It was *her* fault. The last thing they need right now is another baby. He thought she'd moved on from that; he has. He's happy with one child. They can't afford another one anyway – not the way things are. It would mean maternity leave, less money coming in, redecorating the spare room, buying things. And then there were those thoughts he'd had: those fantasies, *sexual* fantasies, about a doll. What if Dianne *does* get pregnant, knowing what he was thinking at the time of conception?

Mrs Lewis on the other hand appears to be in a good mood. She's more affectionate than normal, more attentive. For her, their little 'slip-up' has brought them closer together. It was much needed. She insists on a kiss and a clinch before work. 'You don't regret it, do you?' she says, trying to hold his gaze. 'I can always, you know ... if you're not sure.'

'No, it's fine.' He kisses her perfunctorily, his mind elsewhere. 'I don't really think we should be making a habit of it, though.'

'Oh, I do,' she says, squeezing his bum. Jesus, what's got into her? He can't be doing with it. He wants to be left alone with his misery, his black thoughts and pounding headache.

Preoccupied, he has all but forgotten about the incident at the barbecue. At work, an unexpected mid-morning text from his brother is an unwanted reminder: *Hi buddy. Are things okay? You seemed a bit distracted yesterday.* Shit, he thinks; he was hoping he'd got away with it.

Yes, fine. Why?

Can I call you? Oh God. This sounds serious. His brother doesn't usually call; he's a confirmed texter. Not on a work day either. What's Hayley said to him?

Yes. No worries.

Mr Lewis gets up from his desk to take his phone outside – at the back of the office there's a dingy little concrete yard with sprouting weeds and a lean-to full of signs; too many of them 'sold' ones. His phone rings. He takes a deep breath and answers it. 'Hello.'

'Stephen, how you doing?'

'Yes, I'm good, thanks. Could be a little busier, but you know...'

'That bad, eh?'

'No, it's fine. Things'll pick up.' There's a pause.

'Erm... Thanks for the barbecue yesterday, by the way. It was great. Nice to see everyone.'

'If you wanted to thank me you could have just texted, you know.' He says it as a joke, but is wishing Paul would just come out and say it, get it over and done with.

'Yes, quite. Erm, look, how's things with you and Dianne? Everything OK?'

'Strange question, but yes, good, thanks. We're trying for another baby actually.' Why did he say that? He smacks his forehead. It just came out. But part of it is trying too hard to prove everything is normal.

'Shit. That's brilliant news!' Paul sounds relieved. 'I'll tell Hayley. She'll be thrilled.'

'I'm sure she will. Look, as nice as this is, was there a purpose to this call? I've got *some* work to do, you know.' He laughs.

'Yes, sorry. God, no, I won't keep you. It's just, well, it seems stupid now. I'm actually embarrassed to bring it up...'

'What, for Christ's sake?'

'It's just... Hayley said she thought she heard something yesterday. You know what women are like – two and two makes five and all that. Well, she thought she heard you talking to yourself – or to *someone* – in Lottie's room, calling someone 'princess' and telling her to wake up. Sounds daft, I know, but she was worried about you, that's all. We know things have been a struggle lately – financially and that.' Mr Lewis lets out what he hopes is a convincing laugh before commencing another bout of extemporisation; he's becoming expert at it.

'Oh, Christ. Really? That *is* embarrassing. She probably heard me talking to the cat. She was on Lottie's bed. 'Princess' is my nickname for her. I get a bit soppy with her sometimes – especially when I'm drunk.'

'*Oh my God!*' Paul laughs so hard Mr Lewis has to hold his phone away from his ear. 'Thank fuck for that! We thought you were going nuts! Wait till I tell Hayley – *she'll* be the embarrassed one then.'

Just then Chantelle appears at the back door of the office. She's making a phone signal with her hand and jabbing her thumb in the direction of the office. It looks important.

'Look, Paul, I've got to go. I've got to take a call.'

'Yes, you get on, buddy. I'll catch you later. Good luck with the baby-making!' He's still laughing when Mr Lewis hangs up.

'Mr Gaunt's on the phone. He wants to speak to you,' Chantelle says. Mr Lewis's stomach does cartwheels. This could be it.

'How does he sound?'

'It's hard to say. Fingers crossed, eh?'

It *is* good news, the good news they've been waiting so long to hear. Mr Gaunt wants to go ahead with completion of sale at the reduced price. 'Full steam ahead!' Subject to the mortgage going through in time, he wants a proposed completion date of the second Monday in July – about five weeks from now. Mr Lewis raises a clenched fist as the conversation continues. He looks up at Chantelle and Owen, who are listening with baited breath. They return the gesture, knowing what this means. It's a relief for them too. Owen stands up and does his little victory dance, the one he does every time it looks like a deal's been clinched; it involves pretending he's taking a woman from behind, whilst alternately slapping her bum cheeks with the front and back of his hand. Mr Lewis tries his best to remain calm *and* not to laugh hysterically for the rest of the phone call.

The timescale is ambitious but possibly doable, providing the Simons agree; there's no chain on either side and the property is more or less empty. This is typical of clients: they drag their heels for ever and a day, and then expect the keys to be handed over within days of reaching a decision. You can't rush banks and you can't rush solicitors – Lord knows he's tried over the years. They seem to have a time zone all of their own.

Mr Lewis finally gets off the phone and punches the air again in celebration. '*Yes!*' he shouts. He's such an emotional wreck today, he feels like crying. Hold it together, man. Hold it together. 'Chantelle, get me the Simons' number.'

'Yes, Mr Lewis.'

'Well done, boss. Great news!'

'No, it was a team effort. And let's not get too carried away. You know what it's like – until those contracts are exchanged, anything can happen.'

After phoning the Simons, who, joy of joys, agree to the date in principle, Mr Lewis lets Gaunt know. He feels that old buzz again – the clinching of a deal. He wants to tell Mrs Lewis the good news but she's at work. So he texts her instead: *Good news. We've got a completion date on the Simon house!!!* (three smiley faces *and* a kiss). He presses send. But somehow this doesn't quite satisfy him. He wants to *tell* someone. He wants to tell Eva. How crazy is that? It won't mean a thing to her. But a burden has been lifted and he wants to celebrate, to share it. And he's missing her; he didn't get to see her at all yesterday. He grabs his jacket. 'Take any messages; I'm going out for a bit. I'll be back in an hour.'

'I bet he's going to get Mrs Lewis some flowers,' Chantelle says as he leaves.

As Mr Lewis pulls up on his drive, it hits home what he's doing. Despite the office only being five minutes away, he never normally returns home during the week. He has Mondays for that. Opening his front door and letting himself into the house feels strange. It has a different feel than on Mondays – almost forbidden, as if he's an intruder. The cat, too, seems surprised at Mr Lewis's appearance, eyeing him for longer than usual to make sure it's really him.

Rather than hanging his keys up, he keeps them in his jacket pocket and heads upstairs. Why is he tiptoeing? It's still his house. He wonders if Eva can hear him, or if she knows that it's him. His phone vibrates, making him jump. It's a text from Mrs Lewis: *Brilliant news!!! When is it? Love you. xxx*. He feels a twinge of guilt at this, at what he's doing, at what he's here for, going behind her back; two worlds colliding. He replies before entering the bedroom – trying to keep the two of them separate.

Eva is just as he left her, face down in the toy box having being cast aside in haste. His heart jumps when he sees her: her black hair, blue dress and pale peach skin. He looks longingly at her for a second before picking her up. What is this hold she has over him? Then he wonders what it must be like for her; she must be dying to turn around, right now, to know if it's him. He picks her up. Her body gives straightaway, before she's even facing him. Her eyes blink. 'I knew it was you, Mr Lewis. I could smell you.' Her face is one of wondrous relief and joy. 'What day is it?' She looks confused.

'It's a Tuesday.'

'Gosh, is that all? Every day seems like an eternity. Why aren't you at work? I've been dying to talk to you since the other day when you picked me up.'

'Yesterday, you mean.'

'Yes, yesterday. Sorry. It was so frustrating. You told me you loved me, Mr Lewis. I think you were drunk. You smelt of beer. But I knew someone else was in the house because it didn't feel right; I couldn't change. And I wanted to warn you but couldn't. It wasn't Mrs Lewis, was it? You haven't told her about me, have you?' She grabs his fingers.

'No, no. Don't worry. It was my sister-in-law. It's sorted. I said I was talking to the cat.'

'Oh. What's a sister-in-law?'

'It's not important. Anyway, listen, we've had some good news.' He pops her onto the bed.

'What, me and you, Mr Lewis?'

'No, yes – the family; all of us. A big deal's going through at work. It means we'll have some more money.' Eva looks disappointed.

'Oh. Money's not much use to me, Mr Lewis. Does this mean you'll be less stressed out?'

He laughs at this. 'Yes, perhaps it does.'

'Does that mean we can go out for the day? Me and you?'

'How? How would that be possible?'

'Well, on a Monday.'

Mr Lewis thinks for a moment. 'Even if we could – which I doubt – we don't know if it would work or not. You know, the magic.'

'Well, let's try. Now. Let's try now. Take me outside with you.' She holds up her arms. Just then Mr Lewis's phone goes off in his pocket.

'What's that?' she says.

'My phone. It'll be Dianne.'

'Ignore it, Mr Lewis. Come on, take me outside.'

'I can't. Hold on.' Eva looks put out as he checks the text, and she lowers her arms again. It's nothing that needs replying to. He puts his phone back. Eva's looking up at him with those big eyes, hands clasped together, swaying, as she does when she wants something. He can never resist her; that's his problem.

'Come on then,' he says, offering his hand. She beams and climbs in, wiggling her bum in her satiny dress to get settled.

'You look nice in a suit, Mr Lewis,' she says as he carries her out.

Once they're on the landing, however, she tenses up, clutching his hand. 'Wait. Is that monster down there?'

'Er, yes, actually. I hadn't thought of that.'

'Well, don't put me down whatever you do.'

'Don't worry. You're safe with me. That reminds me, how come you don't change back when Stella's about? Surely she's more of a risk to you than humans?' Eva doesn't answer. She's curled into a ball in his hand.

Mr Lewis turns right at the bottom of the stairs and walks straight into the dining room, so as not to arouse the cat's interest. He walks through the kitchen and into the utility room, closing the door behind him. He pops

Eva on the side next to the washing powder. 'Right. I've no idea how we're going to do this. I must be mad.'

'Imagine what it's like for me, Mr Lewis. I've been waiting for this moment ever since I could move. It could make such a difference to us – there's a whole world out there!'

'But what if it doesn't work? I mean, *I'm* happy the way things are. But I know you'll be disappointed.' He says this, but he's also starting to feel stifled by the limitations of their relationship and what they can do together; in more ways than one. But the thought of being able to take her anywhere he likes, away from the confines of the house, frightens him. Where will it end?

'You have no idea, Mr Lewis. If it doesn't work, it means I'll be trapped in this house forever.' She looks glum, fragile.

'Well, are you really sure you want to find out?'

'Yes. I need to know.'

He spies the washing basket on the floor. 'I've got an idea. Wait a minute. Don't move.' He disappears, closing the door behind him. A few moments later he reappears with some clean towels. He puts one in the bottom of the basket. Picking Eva up, he places her gently on top of it. 'Right, lie down. I'm going to cover you with another towel.' She does as he says, straightening her dress, looking tiny in the basket. 'Now turn on your side, so that you can breathe.' He covers her with another towel.

'It's heavy!' she says, her voice muffled.

'I know. I'll try and be quick.' He kneels down and lifts back the towel. Eva turns to him, shaking. She looks petrified. 'Are you sure you're ready for this?' She nods and bites her lip. 'I'm going to take you out the back door and straight into the shed. The shed's right near the house. If you *can* still move, *don't*. We can't have you wriggling about!' She nods again. 'Right, here goes.' He covers her again.

'Mr Lewis!'

'What?'

'Will you still love me if I can't go outside?'

'Yes, I'll still love you.' He feels like a dumb schoolkid saying it out loud. Picking up the basket, he unlocks the back door and steps outside. It's a warm day, but cool in the shadow of the house. Fortunately their back garden is pretty private: taking a washing basket of towels into a shed might look a bit strange.

Once safely inside, Mr Lewis puts the basket on his work table and closes the door, jamming it shut. He switches on the light. So far there's no movement in the basket. He's disappointed, there's no doubt of this at all. 'Eva, can you still hear me?' No response. Perhaps he needs to touch her again now that they're out of view. Slowly, he pulls back the towel. She's rigid, doll-like, still on her side. He strokes her hair with his thumb, his heart racing; so much depends on this. She stirs, blinks, then reaches out for his hand. Shielding her eyes from the harsh light of the bulb, she turns to look at him. A smile creeps across her face, but it's a sad smile that doesn't quite reach her eyes.

'Hey, what's up? It worked, Eva, it worked! You can move outside!'

'I'm not really outside, am I? I'm in a shed.'

'I know, but you're not in the house.'

'Well, what use is that?'

'It means that it's me you're connected to, not the house. We can go where we like!'

'I turned back, Mr Lewis. Why did I turn back?' She's still lying on her side, looking as if she's about to cry.

'I don't know, perhaps you weren't covered properly or something. Or perhaps someone was looking out of their window.' He rubs her shoulder with his thumb.

'I *was* covered. You know I was!'

'Eva, sit up, look at me.' She slowly sits up on the towel, her knees to the side, her face full of woe. 'I said you might be disappointed, but look – you're outside the house and you're alive! I think that's amazing. It means I can take you places and wake you up.'

'Places like where?'

'I don't know. Places like...' He falters.

'Exactly! I want to paddle in the sea.'

'You'd get swept away!'

'I want to walk amongst bluebells.'

'You'd get eaten by wild animals and stung by nettles.'

'Aaaggh!'

'Look. Perhaps, you're just meant to be an indoor gal, like a precious pet.' He smirks and goes to brush her cheek. She slaps his thumb away.

'Don't joke with me. This isn't funny. I'm nobody's special pet.'

'You are. You're *my* special pet.' He can see her beginning to thaw. But she bangs her fists on the towel in frustration.

'Oh! I so wanted to run in the grass and to go on picnics with you, Mr Lewis.'

'Oh, I can just imagine that. A local estate agent – a father and husband, I hasten to add – sitting on the banks of Rutland Water, having a picnic with a live doll. It would make the front page of the papers! They'd cart me off to the nuthouse. And you – well, they'd probably take you away to be experimented on. You're a marvel of modern science, and a beautiful one at that. We'd probably never see each other again. I think you ought to be thankful for what we've got.' Eva looks serious, but appears to be taking in what he's saying. 'Look, we can still have a picnic somewhere, just an indoor one.'

'When?'

'I don't know. Next Monday, perhaps.'

'Where?'

'I don't know. Somewhere nice.' What was he saying?

'A hotel?'

'Jesus, a hotel? I don't think there are many hotels you can go to for an hour on a Monday morning.'

'Can I get dressed up?'

'Yes, you can get dressed up.'

'Kiss me, Mr Lewis.'

'No, I can't kiss you. It isn't possible.'

'Course it is. Pick me up!' He scoops her up, reluctantly. She's so forward it always makes him shy. He holds her to his chest and she peppers his face with kisses. It's like being pecked by a hummingbird.

'Stop it,' he says, laughing. 'Come on, that's quite enough. We need to go back inside. I should be at work.' Eva groans. He puts her back in the basket. 'Now lie down.' Before he covers her with the second towel, he says: 'I think it's a good thing you can't move outside; you might run away from me.'

'I'll never run away from you, Mr Lewis,' she says, peeking over the towel, her black hair spilling across the lower one. 'I wish you could join me in here. It's like a cosy bed.'

'Shush now.' She sticks her tongue out at him and he covers her up, smiling.

Experiment over, and back in Lottie's room, Eva grows solemn again. She always does when it's time to say goodbye. 'It's all right for you, Mr Lewis; you've got Lottie and Mrs Lewis. I've got no one. I get lonely.' Mr Lewis promises there will be plenty more days ahead – especially after what they've just discovered. It's been a red letter day, one that has given him food for thought. He just needs to figure out how to harness the new information, that's all.

CHAPTER 10

June is a mixed salad of a month for Mr Lewis; full of promise and colour but ultimately unfulfilling. It starts off well. The buoyancy of the sale being agreed seems to have a knock-on effect at work. Things start to pick up a bit: more viewings, a couple of surveys (to keep David happy), another agreed sale subject to contract (and another victory dance from Owen). He keeps in regular contact with Gaunt and the Simons. No problems. The mortgage is going through (slowly). It's always a testing time, a nervous time. The Simons want contracts to be exchanged as soon as possible, so the deal is done; Mr Lewis too. Then everyone will be able to relax a little. Mr Gaunt, true to form, wants to wait. He has to give a month's notice on his and his wife's current rental property, and he won't do that until the mortgage is signed off.

As for Eva, Mr Lewis now dedicates his Mondays fully to her. An hour every Wednesday evening too. This has become part of his routine. Anything else in between is a bonus. He wonders where he can take her: he needs a roof, a building, an enclosed space that isn't public. He's not going to start booking himself into hotels; that would be madness. He can't afford it for a start. And what if someone recognises him? Wait a minute! At the office he has the keys to maybe half a dozen properties around town – one of them unoccupied (for the time being): the big one; the Simons' residence. It is perfect; totally unethical, but perfect.

On the planned day out, he is ludicrously excited. Once his wife and Lottie have gone, he wakes Eva up. She can also barely contain herself, and drags the tin over to the toy box. 'What are you doing?' he asks.

'I'm getting changed. I want to look nice. And then I've got to get packed. I need a suitcase and spare clothes.'

'Eva, we're only going for an hour or so. It's not a weekend away!'

'Well, you never know. A girl always needs a change of clothes.'

Mr Lewis sighs. 'I'll leave you to it then, but hurry up. We haven't got long. I've got to get the picnic ready.'

Half an hour later they're ready to leave. Mr Lewis feels nervous. This is a big operation. First he's got to collect the keys from the office. How does he explain this? They've got to be signed for as well. He'll think of something. Eva will have to go in his briefcase – along with the picnic items and her suitcase. If he meets with a fatal accident before he reaches his destination, these contents will make for some interesting future discussions. Eva is none too happy about her mode of transport. He reminds her she'll be asleep.

Or so he thinks.

As he drives to the office, he's taken aback by a sudden wailing from the briefcase. 'Eva? Why aren't you asleep?'

She answers in a muffled voice. 'I don't know, but I don't like it! My tummy feels funny and I keep sliding about! Can't you drive slower?'

'I'm not driving fast. Can't you get in a pocket or something?'

'I'll try!'

When he pulls up outside the office, he hears her again: 'Thank God for that! Are we there? Can I get out yet?'

'No. I'm at the office – I've got to get the keys.' Eva groans. The window of the car is slightly open, and just at that moment a man with a dog walks past. He gives Mr Lewis a funny look. Mr Lewis coughs and puts a hand up in greeting. 'Eva! You've got to be quiet!' he hisses when the man has passed. 'I'll be back in a few minutes.'

'Sorry. Hurry up though; it smells in here because of the food.' He makes sure he shuts the window and locks the car, carefully putting the briefcase under the seat for good measure.

Ten minutes later, and after another bout of wailing, later, he's parked on the street of the Simon residence, a safe distance from it. The beauty of the property is that it's on a fairly busy street; if it was on a quiet one or in a village he would be conspicuous. Besides, he's been to the house maybe a dozen times over the past twelve months: no one will bat an eyelid at him entering it with a briefcase.

Mr Lewis lets himself in, feeling a little guilty. It's cool inside. His shoes clip-clop on the parquet floor and echo in the spacious hallway. He heads upstairs.

Once he's on the first-floor landing, he kneels down to unlock the briefcase. Eva is starting to get impatient again. 'Mr Lewis! Are we there yet?'

'Yes, just a minute.' He adjusts the combination numbers. Clunk-clunk: the brass locks flip open. He carefully puts the case down and opens it. This is another milestone moment. Will the magic work in another house? What if she goes back to sleep?

He needn't have worried: Eva is standing in a pleated burgundy pocket, next to some pens. She looks a little queasy, but is wide awake. He breathes a sigh of relief. 'Are we really there?' she says. Mr Lewis nods. A smile lights up her face. He sets her down on the carpet. She stretches, screams in delight, then goes running down the landing. 'Sshh!' he says – not that anyone can hear. He smiles too, to see her so happy.

There's so much for Eva to explore. She hops, skips, jumps and cartwheels from room to room, asking Mr Lewis to chase after her. Eventually she wears him out, and he tells her he's setting up the picnic. She finds him in a large and empty front room with huge windows. She walks straight past him and ducks under a net curtain to peer at the buildings opposite; fortunately empty business premises that are to let. Even so, someone could look up from the street. 'Eva, come back, you'll get me shot,' Mr Lewis says. 'Come and sit down. I've got something for you.' He reaches into his jacket pocket.

Eva trots over and sits down. 'Here. Forget-me-nots to go with your blue dress and daisies to go with your white one. You can't go outside, so I wanted to bring the outside in.' He passes her the flowers; tiny in his fingers, a perfect bouquet in her hand.

'Thank you. That's so thoughtful.' She puts the flowers down, then plucks out a forget-me-not and places it in her hair.

'Now, let's eat. I missed breakfast.'

Picture the scene: huge windows in a high-ceilinged room, a grown man in a business suit sitting cross-legged on the floor, a briefcase by his side. Opposite him is a living doll, a miniature human, perfect in every way, kneeling with her legs demurely to the side. A check tablecloth is between them, dotted with miniature titbits and crockery. They talk and eat and laugh as if it's the most normal thing in the world.

Afterwards Mr Lewis sheds his jacket, loosens his tie and lies on his back on the floor. He feels a freedom that he couldn't possibly achieve at home. He stretches his arms out in a cross, feeling like Gulliver, whilst Lilliputian Eva runs amok on his body; a form of massage – like those little fish that nibble your feet.

They explore the house together, playing hide and seek. On the next floor is an attic room, full of furniture covered in sheets. It has a rear window onto a courtyard garden, all lavender and sunshine. He sits Eva on the sill, so she can look out. He opens the window for her, letting the outside in again, but she immediately turns back into a doll. This would explain why she changed back when Stella flew out through the cat flap on that rainy day – not because she was scared. He's discovering new things about her all the time. Mr Lewis wakes her up and calls her his 'little vampire' – she can't walk in

Eva: A grown-up fairy tale

the sun and she'll never grow old. It's soon time to go home.

That evening Mr Lewis is satisfied with himself and his day's work. His briefcase has been emptied. Everything has been put back and cleared away, including Eva. It's been a success. He's being meticulous in covering his duplicity, his double life. He knows how to keep things separate, how to cover his tracks – especially after his early mistakes.

In reality, however, he's taking more and more risks, blinded by love, becoming more and more addicted. He's preoccupied with finding miniature things for Eva. In the kitchen drawer there's a treasure trove of leftover items from Christmas crackers – some tiny playing cards (for their next day out), a pack of mini-pencils and notepad ('Teach me to read and write, Mr Lewis'), miniature screwdrivers (what would she even need them for?), a mini-Bible from an arcade machine. He stores them all in his briefcase, changing the combination on it.

The way he sees it, she's his little oasis in a humdrum world, his little secret, his release. She's his mistress, his plaything, his shoulder to cry on. It's become an affair in every aspect, except for the main one – sex. And this is possibly what drives him on; the fact that their relationship hasn't been consummated. But how could it be? To say they're physically incompatible is the understatement of the century; no, the millennium.

This doesn't stop Mr Lewis from tormenting himself. She loves to dress up and dance for him – and boy is she flexible, doing the splits with ease. Different outfits, different colours, different ribbons and bows in her hair

– hula girl (his favourite), air hostess, a Union Jack mini-dress that barely covers her bum, '80s chick; a fantasy world. He loves to watch her; he's given up pretending otherwise.

They become more familiar with each other, Mr Lewis less inhibited. He stays in the bathroom whilst she's bathing. He helps to wash her hair, squeezing a sponge over it to wash the soap away whilst she leans her head back, her breasts bobbing on the water. He shaves under her arms for her with his wife's safety razor, holding her little wrist in the air, not trusting her to do it herself. He stops short of touching her, though, or letting her touch him – in that way anyhow. Not that she doesn't ask for it; she says she aches for him 'down there'. And he aches for her.

But it's not all plain sailing; far from it. Eva's normally cheerful disposition becomes increasingly peppered with mood swings and waspish outbursts. And then, as with most mistresses, it's not long before jealousy rears its ugly head, like a little black spider in the corner of the room that has grown bloated and fat – fed on indignation.

One day, an opportunistic Friday morning before work, she's in a bad mood from the second she's woken up. 'Why do you always say "Eva, wake up"? I'm not asleep. I can still see and hear, remember.'

'Sorry, sometimes I forget.'

'I don't like Mrs Lewis,' she says.

'What a ridiculous thing to say; you don't even know her.'

'I don't like her whiny voice. She's always nagging at you and Lottie.'

'Well, we're all just a bit on edge, I suppose, until this deal goes through.'

'Why are you sticking up for her? I heard you two last night, you know.' Ah, so that explains it. 'I couldn't stand it. I couldn't even cover my ears – do you know how frustrating that is?'

'That's interesting; it wasn't so long ago you found it amusing.'

'Well, things have changed.' They certainly had.

'Look, if it it's any consolation I didn't enjoy it. It's my wife ... she wants another baby.'

'Oh, please!' says Eva.

'It's true.'

'Well it's not fair. If you were a cake, Mr Lewis, she'd be getting the cream, the icing *and* the cherry on top! And I just get the crumbs!'

After this conversation, the next time he and his wife make love (at Mrs Lewis's behest), it becomes even harder for Mr Lewis to perform, as he knows Eva might be listening. It's as if she's done it on purpose. He feels tense. He becomes aware of his wife's body underneath him. She feels so ... well, big. And she smells so strong and cloying – perfume, hairspray, moisturiser, toothpaste, washing powder; all chemicals, all man-made artificial fragrances. He feels as if he's drowning in an olfactory ocean. Eva, in comparison, smells of nothing but hair and skin, a little light musk from her armpits – all her own intoxicating perfume. How ironic is that? She's the doll, yet she smells more natural.

On Friday, at the end of the working week, Mr Lewis is the last to leave the office. He's already thinking ahead to Monday. Before locking up, he removes the Simon keys from the drawer they're kept in, numbered and labelled with all the others, and puts them in his briefcase. He could hardly go in the office on Monday morning and claim he has to go to the house again. Relocking the drawer, he tells himself this is the last time he can use it; people on the street will start to notice – besides, any week now the Simons will be back themselves to clear out any last items; he could do with checking that so he doesn't get caught out.

The following Monday morning he lets himself into the property again. This time he kneels down in the hallway to open his briefcase, thinking he'll let Eva have a run around downstairs for a change. He can't wait to get her out and she can't wait to *get* out; she's already hammering on the case and hollering. As he adjusts the numbers on the locks, telling Eva to be quiet as he remembers the new combination, something suddenly comes to him – an ingenious idea; a lightbulb moment. Combinations, numbers ... why hasn't he thought of it before? What if there's a combination to make Eva grow? The same size as him? She's magic, right? She's unlocked sight, smell, hearing and movement: what if she can make herself bigger? It's a quixotic notion, and no doubt a selfish one, but she's a living, breathing doll for Christ's sake. Who knows what she can achieve? He has to tell her right away, while they've got the opportunity. This could be the last time.

He opens the case. Eva has fallen out of her perch and is lying amongst all manner of miniature items he's brought. She's squinting at the light and not looking too happy. 'That's the last time I'm coming here in this thing – awake anyway. You'll have to think of something else!'

'All right, all right,' he says, plucking her out. 'Eva, listen to me...'

'Wait a minute, let me get my bearings. Put me down.' She brushes herself down and rubs her eyes. 'It's so dark in that briefcase. I hate it.' Mr Lewis watches her, his mind turning over, imagining what she would look like if she were the same size as him. Gorgeous, no doubt – she was perfect in every way. How tall would she be?

'Are you ready? You've got to listen to me, Eva, I've got an idea.'

'Sounds interesting.'

'Now I know this might sound crazy, but hear me out... What if you could make yourself big? Not big but, you know, the same size as me?'

'How?'

'With one of your combinations – the numbers.' It was something they'd never really discussed.

'I'm not sure if that would work.'

'Why not? I mean, I don't know how any of this works – how the magic works – but look what you've unlocked already. There could be a combination for anything ... maybe even going outside. Who knows?'

Her eyes light up at this. 'There could be! Now that *would* be worth unlocking!'

'Well, let's not get carried away just yet or get sidetracked – let's stick to the growing thing.' If he was being perfectly honest, the fact that Eva couldn't go outside suited him; she'd only be constantly pestering him about it – and it was far too risky, a recipe for disaster.

'Why? What's with making me big all of a sudden? Don't you like me the way I am?' She strikes one of her poses.

'Course I do. You know I do, but you know...'

'No, tell me. What's on your mind, you naughty man?' She walks over and puts a little foot on one of his huge brogues, leaning on her knee and looking up at him. Mr Lewis can't look her in the eye.

'Nothing. It would just make things easier, that's all.' She begins playing with his laces, toying with them, wrapping them round her tiny hand and wrist.

'Easier for what?'

'Come on, Eva, don't make me say it.'

'You want to do it with me, don't you, Mr Lewis? Like you do with Mrs Lewis.'

'*Eva!*' He blushes, but it's almost a relief to have it out in the open, to actually acknowledge it. He scoops her up. 'You just drive me crazy, that's all.' He nuzzles her nose.

'Good,' she says. 'So when do we start?'

'Well, now, I guess, whilst we've got time.'

Mr Lewis shuts his briefcase and carries her upstairs. They sit down by the fireplace in one of the large drawing rooms. 'Right then, how does it work?'

'Well, it's been a while since I've done it, so I might be a bit rusty. Once I could move, you see, I stopped. There was nothing else I wanted – or so I thought. And that was different again, because I still needed you to trigger that. I still do. But I knew I'd unlocked it. I can feel this sort of vibration, like a humming through me, when I'm getting close. It takes a lot of concentration and a lot of time – unless I get lucky – so don't expect anything to happen just like that. Basically, I have to try different numbers in different sequences; always six numbers and no higher than the number nine. And I have to wish for what I want too. The only reason I came across this at all was because I used to be so bored. I started arranging digits in different orders in my mind, which I realise now was quite a scary place, just blank darkness. I didn't even know how to say the numbers because I couldn't hear; they were just forms or shapes in random order. One day, purely by chance, I unlocked hearing. I'll never forget it. Once I could hear, though, there was no stopping me. I started doing it methodically, putting the numbers to rhythms or beats: *zero, zero, zero – zero, zero, one, pause, zero, zero, zero – zero, zero, two, pause, zero, zero, zero – zero, zero, three*. And so on all the way up to nine. Then I'd do *zero, zero, zero – zero, one, one, pause, zero, zero, zero – zero, one, two*. And on and on.'

'But how did you remember the combinations? If you couldn't write them down, say?'

'I didn't have to. Once they were unlocked that was it.'

'So you haven't used the same combinations twice?

'Not that I know of. I've had no need to. I wouldn't even know what they were now?' Something about this concerns Mr Lewis. What if they needed to reverse the combination, for example, to make her small again – which they *would* have to do?

'So you've never tried reversing any of the combinations either?'

'No. Even if I could remember them, why would I want to? They might not work again.'

'No reason. I think it would be sensible if we write this one down, though, if you unlock it. Just in case.' He opens up the briefcase, pulls out the little notepad and pencils, and passes them to her.

'I haven't learnt to write yet, Mr Lewis. You're meant to teach me, remember?'

'Oh yes. Well, it's just numbers, just writing what you see.' There's silence for a moment.

'So, are you going to try?'

'Don't pressure me or I won't be able to focus.'

'Sorry.'

Eva lies down on her back and closes her eyes. Her chest rises and falls. A few minutes pass. Mr Lewis looks at his watch. The sound disturbs Eva. She sits up.

'I can't concentrate, knowing you're watching me. I feel under pressure. It's weird, but when I did it before I couldn't move. Now I can feel my heart beating; I can feel my chest breathing. It makes it harder. *And* you're being noisy.'

'Do you want me to leave for a bit?'

Eva frowns. 'Surely the purpose of coming here was so we can be together? I can't be bothered with this.'

'Yes, but if this works we can *really* be together, properly. Give it another fifteen minutes. I'll have a wander for a bit.'

'Can I have a drink first? I'm thirsty.' He pours her a little cup of water.

'Thank you.'

'You don't have to start from the zeros again, do you?' Mr Lewis says before he leaves.

'No. I know I got up to at least the fours when I unlocked movement. So I'm starting from there.'

'Right. I'll leave you to it.'

Mr Lewis wanders the semi-empty building. The place looks even bigger unfurnished. It makes him wonder what Gaunt's going to do with such a big house. Mr

Lewis has only met Mrs Gaunt twice – for the two first viewings – a little bird of a woman; the total opposite of Mr Gaunt. They certainly didn't appear to have any children living with them. It's probably a status symbol – somewhere to host vast parties. As he walks about, he keeps on hoping to hear a shout from upstairs. He fantasises about finding a fully grown woman on the floor, and throwing himself upon her, finally able to have her.

It doesn't happen. And after a quarter of an hour or so he returns to the drawing room. Eva is still on her back. She doesn't hear him come in and appears to be in a catatonic state, almost like a doll but still human. Perhaps she's fallen asleep. 'Eva?' he says. She twitches to life, looking disappointed and tired.

'No joy?'

'No, but I *was* able to concentrate. I forgot how much it takes out of you. It seems to sap your energy. More so now that I'm moving. It's just going to take time. That's if it works at all. Perhaps there's nothing else for me to unlock.'

'Maybe,' he says. Perhaps it was a stupid idea; wishful thinking. 'What do you want to do now? A game of cards?'

'No, I just want you to hold me for a while.' Mr Lewis lies on the floor on his back, propping his head on his briefcase and jacket for a pillow. It's a shame this place hasn't got a bed. Eva clambers onto his chest and lies down under his chin. She moves up and down with his breathing. It feels nice, so nice he could nod off for a bit...

There's the bang of a door slamming downstairs. Mr Lewis sits bolt upright in alarm, instinctively clutching

Eva to him. She's gone stiff. What the hell? He'd dropped off to sleep. He hears voices echoing in the hallway. His skin contracts and his heart appears to stop beating. *Jesus Christ! There's someone in the house!*

He jumps up, grabbing his briefcase and jacket, his hair sticking up at the back. The voices seem to be getting louder, posh voices, a man and a woman's. They're coming up the stairs. Mr Lewis spins round in panic, desperately searching for somewhere to hide. There are no curtains, nothing. He can hear their footsteps on the landing. *Oh fuck, oh fuck, oh fuck! I'm done for. I've had it!* He looks down at his left hand, still clutching Eva; he hasn't had time to put her back in his briefcase. The footsteps are getting closer, and he darts behind the door, his back pressed to the wall. He can barely breathe. His chest feels tight. *Please don't have a heart attack, not now. Not like this.* He thinks of the shame it would bring on his family. He thinks of how Lottie would be teased at school. *I'm sorry, Dianne, I'm sorry, Lottie.* The people pass the room he's in.

'We'll have to hire a skip, I suppose…' a man's voice says. The voice is familiar. It's Mr Simon! Mr Lewis hears the creak of more stairs. They're going up to the next floor. Their voices become muffled. Just then his phone vibrates; it's in his jacket pocket. He grabs it. It's the office calling. *Shit!* He presses a button in panic. The footsteps falter.

'What?' Mr Simon says. Mr Lewis holds his breath. A bead of sweat trickles down the side of his face, tickling him.

'Did you just hear something?'
'No, why?'

'I thought I heard something, a buzzing.'
'Must be the ghost!'
'Oh don't, Percy! This place always gave me the creeps!' Their footsteps start again. Mr Lewis exhales, and edges out from behind the door on tiptoe. He peers round the doorway onto the landing – a trespasser with unkempt hair in a pale blue shirt, sweat patches under his armpits, clutching a briefcase and a black-haired doll. He darts across the landing and down the stairs. In the hallway, he quickly dons his jacket and flicks open his briefcase to shove Eva in. All the while, he looks up the stairs. Then, as quietly as he can, he opens the front door and lets himself out. 'Morning!' a passerby says cheerfully.

'Morning,' he replies, mopping his brow.

'Warm, isn't it?'

Mr Lewis grimaces and scurries off in the opposite direction.

Back in the safety of his car, he plonks his briefcase on the passenger seat and lets out a huge rush of breath. Putting his head back on the headrest, he notices something on his windscreen. Tucked under the wiper is a parking ticket.

CHAPTER 11

The narrow escape is a wake-up call for Mr Lewis. He's putting his family in jeopardy. It's time to pull back a bit. He *thought* he was being meticulous, but, inevitably, juggling so many balls – work, Eva, the Gaunt–Simon deal, his family – things are beginning to slip through the net. When he's unloading his briefcase, he discovers that he can't find the miniature notepad and pencils. Has he left them at the Simons' house? Has he got to go back and get them? He's also still got the Simons' keys. On top of all this, there's the small matter of that parking ticket to deal with.

Mrs Lewis is also starting to notice a few things; prompted mainly by her husband's lack of interest in the bedroom. He seems distant in general – preoccupied. Today, on her morning break, she rings him at home and at work; he isn't in either place. 'Must be out on a viewing,' she says to Chantelle.

'Oh, I don't think there are any today, Mrs Lewis. Try his mobile.'

Instead of doing this, Mrs Lewis casually asks him when she gets home from work, 'Any viewings today?'

'No,' he replies.

Where had he been then? She doesn't question him on it; just mentally stores it away. She checks the messages on his phone (something she had never done before) – he never deletes them, doesn't even have a pass code – but there is nothing incriminating.

****

June rolls into July. The Gaunts' mortgage has gone through and they have finally handed in their rental notice. Contracts, however, are still yet to be exchanged – solicitors the delay this time. The knock-on effect of this is that it sets the completion date back a week or so. Out of all the parties concerned, Mrs Lewis is the least pleased about this. The completion of the deal – handing over keys, money transfer – could run into their annual holiday. This year, as every year, they have the same static caravan booked in Great Yarmouth for the first week of the school summer holidays; another tradition, and the only guaranteed holiday they get these days. It was a friend of a friend's and ridiculously cheap – a home from home, and only two-and-a-half hours away.

What annoys Mrs Lewis the most is her husband's casual attitude towards this. 'Oh, never mind. If it happens, you and Lottie just go on ahead… I'll meet you out there when the deal's done.'

'But it won't be the same going without you. This is our family holiday!'

'Well, take your sister and her kids with you for a few days. Lottie'll have a great time with her cousins – and you know I only get in the way of you and your sister!'

Despite Mr Lewis trying to rein things in where he and Eva are concerned, he can't help but see this as the perfect, selfish opportunity he's been so craving; the whole house for just the two of them. Instead of hoping that the completion of the sale doesn't get in the way of the family holiday; he's actually hoping it does. He's certainly not going to put pressure on to try and force things, despite the Simons' insistence. If only she can make herself bigger in time. He asks her how this is going.

'It's slow progress, Mr Lewis – and exhausting. I can only do it for so long.'

'Anything at all? Any "vibrations" as you call them?'

'Not yet, I'm afraid… Anyway, I miss you, Mr Lewis. I want to go out. We haven't been out for ages.'

'I know. Me too. We will soon – I've got a surprise for you.'

'Oh what is it, Mr Lewis?! Tell me, please!'

'You'll have to wait and see. Just keep crunching those numbers!'

****

Mr Lewis regularly wakes Eva up on a Monday, hoping that every time she'll have some good news for him, or maybe turn instantly into a fully grown woman. She doesn't.

But in the week leading up to the end of the school term, the third week in July, things begin to happen. Eva is in a state of excitement. She's into the sixes now and can start to feel some vibrations. They're getting stronger. Mr Lewis can't believe it. He's on tenterhooks all week. As Friday morning, the proposed completion day, arrives, he's a bag of nerves. Contracts have been exchanged; all that is needed is for the banks to do their bit; then the keys can be handed over. Mrs Lewis puts her husband's mood down to his desperation for the money to arrive. It's the opposite: he's praying that it doesn't. 'Ring them up, ring them up, see what's happening!' she says. The Gaunts and the Simons keep ringing too. The three o'clock deadline comes and goes. It's going to be Monday. Everyone is disappointed; everyone except Mr Lewis.

That evening the Lewises pack for their holiday, ready to depart in the morning. It's a strange time. Mrs Lewis is deflated, disappointed. Although her husband has shown no outer signs of anything suspicious, there's something about the prospect of going away without him, or more to the point leaving him alone for the weekend, that bothers her. Mr Lewis, in contrast, is cheerful and relaxed – content in the knowledge that the deal is pretty much done and dusted, and more to the point that he's got his wish: his alone time with Eva. The best of both worlds.

He dedicates his time to his family – his wife and daughter. He goes to the shops with them instead of staying at home. Holiday items are bought: suncream, sunglasses, toiletries, a new windbreak, a bottle of champagne to celebrate with. The truth is, he doesn't trust himself. What if he's tempted to wake Eva? What if she grows larger? What if he can't make her shrink again? Put the genie back in the bottle, so to speak? This close, he daren't risk it. It could ruin everything. Mrs Lewis has to go and pick up the keys for the caravan, so he suggests eating out to save her cooking; somewhere not too expensive. 'We can pick up the keys on the way,' he says. It feels more like old times.

CHAPTER 12

Saturday morning arrives. Mrs Lewis's sister and her children turn up early, ready for the journey, as arranged. 'Hi, Uncle Stephen!' They run upstairs to play. After a cup of tea, and much stress and commotion, they are all crammed into two cars. Mr Lewis jokes with his sister-in-law not to get too comfortable; he should be there by Monday evening. He kisses and hugs his wife and tells her to put that bottle of champagne on ice. Waving them off, he feels a pang of guilt as Lottie waves excitedly back at him from the rear seat. She's surrounded by bedding and clutching her tablet.

Mr Lewis closes the door and runs upstairs. He charges into his daughter's room and goes straight to the toy box. He simply can't wait, or imagine what's in store for them both; this could be 'the moment'...

Eva isn't in the box.

What the hell? She was definitely there last night. He frantically rummages through the box on his hands and knees, throwing toys out. Why didn't he think of this? Why didn't he ask Lottie what she was taking? Why didn't he pay more attention? This could be a disaster. Eva definitely isn't there. 'No! No-no-no! Don't tell me she's taken her with her!' he cries in anguish. This can't be happening! He grabs his hair, wanting to pull it out in clumps.

Desperately, he searches the room – the floor, the bed; he looks down the side of it, underneath it, lifts up the mattress. Nothing. His phone goes off downstairs. On the verge of tears, he ignores it.

Nausea takes hold of him; he feels as if he's going to be sick – sick with disappointment. He yanks open Lottie's drawers, rifling through them, but still no sign of Eva. He lurches over to the wardrobe, flinging open the door, pulling out clothes; sometimes Lottie shoves toys in there as a way of tidying up her bedroom. Still nothing.

Mr Lewis sinks to his knees in despair, and holds his head in his hands. He should be with his family; the thought of being stuck here for the whole weekend, alone now, is horrific; he's even arranged to have the morning off work. He feels racked with guilt. Downstairs, he hears his phone go again. Who the hell can it be? What's so important?ND, he gets to his feet and makes his way downstairs.

There are two missed calls from Mrs Lewis. Guilt again. What if they've broken down or forgotten something? He calls her back straight away. Mrs Lewis answers; she's on speaker phone. 'Hi, Daddy!' he hears Lottie shout in the background.

'Hi, honey. What's up? Everything OK?'

'Yes, fine. I just forgot to remind you. Can you ring Nicky – I forgot to tell her you're there for the weekend. She's coming tomorrow to feed the cat. We won't need her till Tuesday now – hopefully not anyway.'

'Yes, sure. No problem.' It's a good job she *did* remember, he thinks. Who knows what he could have been doing tomorrow? But then it hits him that he won't be doing *anything* tomorrow – Eva. He groans inside when he remembers. It crosses his mind to ask Lottie where the doll is, or if she's taken her. But how would he explain that? Why would he be asking? He wishes them a safe trip (again) – telling them he loves them – and hangs up, feeling miserable. He wishes he was with them.

The phone call has sobered him up, at least, and enables him to think more clearly. What if Eva is here and he's just missed her? Imagine getting to Norfolk on Monday and finding out she was in the house all along; that would be even worse. 'Think, think,' he says to himself. The kids were playing in Lottie's room before they left. An idea comes to him. There's one place left that he hasn't looked. He dashes upstairs.

On the floor, next to the toy box, is the metal camouflage tin. He hadn't paid it any attention before, hadn't thought of it; it's his last hope.

He crouches down on one knee and picks up the tin, giving it a shake. Something rattles inside and his heart flutters. He says a little a prayer and slowly prises open the lid. A flash of a familiar colour – a shiny bright blue – catches his eye. It's Eva's dress.

Mr. Lewis throws the lid wide open. Inside, Eva is in a faux-loving embrace with the army doll, their arms around each other and their faces pressed together. The kids must have put them like this – that or she's cheating on him. Mr Lewis feels like weeping again, but this time in pure joy and relief. He doesn't pick her up, just stares at her, feeling spent. He strokes her little satiny blue dress, enjoying the feel of the silky texture between his thumb and forefinger. He touches her hair and she begins to stir, begins to soften, begins to change.

Her big eyes blink and she's awake. She immediately pulls a face. 'Ugh! Get your filthy mitts off me!' She pushes down the army doll's arms and shoves him away, wiping her mouth with the back of her hand. Mr Lewis laughs. She turns to face him. 'Get me out of here, Mr Lewis.'

He picks her up, her little waist tiny and familiar in his hand. 'So, how long has this been going on behind my back?' he says, smiling.

'Hardly. Those brats put me in here. Lottie should know better. It was horrible, Mr Lewis. I thought they were going to take me with them. Him, too. I heard them discussing it.'

'You know then – about them going away?'

'Course I know – you lot have been talking about it for days. I thought you were going to go without me.'

'Oh. That's a shame. It was going to be my little surprise. I thought you would think it was Monday today.'

'Well, sorry to disappoint you. But that doesn't matter now. Have we really got the weekend to ourselves, Mr Lewis? Just me and you?' She puts her face against his thumb and hugs it tight.

'We sure have, well, me, you and the cat. And that reminds me; I've got to give Nicky a ring.'

Eva groans. 'Who's he?'

'Nicky's a she. She feeds the cat when we're away.' Mr Lewis gets out his phone and scrolls through his contacts. He doesn't have her number. 'Must be in the phonebook,' he says.

'So, what are we going to do, Mr Lewis? Can we go out for the day?'

'There's probably no point – not with having the house to ourselves.' Eva looks disappointed. He sits her down on the bed and strokes her hair. 'Maybe tomorrow. Besides, we've got more pressing business. You need to try and make yourself big, remember. The sooner we start the better.' He'd been so happy just to see Eva; it hadn't bothered him at first that she'd not grown yet. But that *was* the whole point of this alone time. Eva tuts.

'Is that all you think about, Mr Lewis? I've been trying, you know.'

'Well, I thought you'd be as keen as me. You know, with the house to ourselves and that...' He gives her a look.

'I am, it's just...'

'Just what?'

'I'm scared. I mean, what if it goes wrong? What if I get damaged or disfigured? What if you don't love me any more? Or what if I can't go back again?'

'Hey, I should be more worried about that than you!' he laughs. 'Course I'll still love you, I might love you even more!'

'That doesn't make me feel much better.'

'Come on. Enough talking. We're wasting time, stuck in here. You're the lady of the house now!'

'I am actually, aren't I?' Eva says, brightening, and slips off the bed.

After doing a window check and locking the cat flap, Mr Lewis calls her downstairs. They have a bit of breakfast together, watch a bit of telly. Eva enjoys the relaxation, the run of the house, the lack of pressure. Mr Lewis reads the paper whilst Eva wanders about. She climbs up to look longingly out of different windows, until Mr Lewis has to tell her to come away. She stares out of the patio doors instead. Unlike Eva, he's all too aware of the clock ticking. Before they know it, the weekend will be over. He starts to feel restless.

Getting up from the sofa, Mr Lewis walks over to scoop her up. 'Come on, it's time,' he says. Eva looks resigned, but also a little scared.

'Can I have a bath first? I want to be clean, you know, for when – for if it happens.'

'Sure you can, honeybunch.'

She snuggles into his palm. 'I like it when you call me names.'

Mr Lewis puts Eva on the back of the bathroom basin, then goes to turn on the hot tap.

'Wait!' she cries, looking awkward.

'What?'

'Er... I think I need to go to the toilet first.' This seems to be the only thing that she gets embarrassed about – as if she finds it distasteful.

'But how...'

She cuts him off. 'I'll deal with it. Just leave me to it.'

'Well, if you're sure. But call me when you need the bath running.'

'It's OK. I'll manage. I've got to learn to do these things myself. Just loosen the taps for me before you go. Oh, and unscrew the lid on the bubblebath. Put it next to the taps, please.' Mr Lewis does as she asks, reminding her to be careful, then leaves her to it.

Back downstairs, as before, he tries not to think about what's going on in there. He tries to do the crossword to take his mind off it. After a few minutes he can hear the taps being turned on, which amuses him. It *is* nice to have the house to themselves. It's nice not to have to go into work on a Saturday for once as well. He begins to relax a little again and puts some music on. But not too loud, in case Eva needs him.

****

Eva has finished her bath and calls Mr Lewis up. He feels a tingle of anticipation as he heads upstairs. She's standing on the back of the now empty basin, looking pleased with herself, a white flannel tucked around her. The floor around the basin is soaking wet. 'I see you've managed to get out yourself this time?' he says.

'Yes. I let the basin fill and just floated to the top!'

'You are a clever girl, aren't you?' He picks her up. Her skin temperature has changed. She feels warmer in his hand.

'I know. Look, I've even shaved my legs myself.' She holds one out for inspection. 'Feel it, Mr Lewis.' He runs his forefinger along her little shin. It's perfectly smooth. She shudders unexpectedly at his touch and their eyes meet briefly. Mr Lewis looks away.

'Can I get my hairbrush from Lottie's room?' she says.

'Sure.' He carries her out of the bathroom, glad of the distraction.

Eva: A grown-up fairy tale

'No, put me down. I can do it.' She totters off along the landing, her little bum wiggling nonchalantly in her towel. Queen Bee. She leaves tiny wet footprints on the carpet. Mr Lewis watches after her and smiles in wonder. He goes to mop up the bathroom floor.

When she returns, Mr Lewis is sitting on his bed, waiting for her. She stands at the doorway, brushing her hair with a little dark pink brush – all so natural. Her hair's straight, impossibly black. 'Does this mean I'm sleeping in here tonight?' she says as she enters the room, not taking her eyes off him. All Mr Lewis can do is gulp. She holds her arms up to be put on the bed. Mr Lewis obliges.

Putting her hairbrush on the bedside table – on Mrs Lewis's side – Eva lies back on the pillow. She's staring at the ceiling. 'I guess this is it then,' she says, turning to him.

'I guess it is… You never know; it might not work.'

'It might not. I was getting close to something, though, I could feel it.'

'What *does* it feel like?'

'Do you want me to show you?' Mr Lewis nods. She curls her hand around his little finger and pulls his hand towards her. 'Put your hand across me.' He does as she says. Eva lies back, arms by her side, facing upwards, and closes her eyes.

Mr Lewis waits. For a minute he can't feel anything. He doesn't know what he's meant to be feeling. Eva's face has a look of extreme concentration on it. She's frowning slightly, her eyes screwed tight. All of a sudden, he starts to feel an undeniable humming or vibration under his hand. It's coming from Eva's body. Slowly but surely, it starts to get stronger until it tickles his hand. It feels like he's holding an electric toothbrush. Then the vibrating stops abruptly and Eva opens her eyes.

'Could you feel it?' Mr Lewis nods, amazed. 'It's getting stronger. You need to go now.'

'Why?'

'Because I don't want you to be around if it happens. I don't want you to see.' Mr Lewis gets up from the bed. He kisses his index finger and puts it to her forehead. She clings on to it as he leaves, that worried look on her face again. It makes Mr Lewis feel worried too – guilty as he closes the door on her. What if something *does* go wrong? Should he be making her do this? Was it fair? Only time will tell. He feels like a drink...

CHAPTER 13

Mr Lewis has just finished replying to a text from his wife. They've all arrived at the caravan, safe and sound. Lottie and the kids are already in the open air pool at the complex, and Mrs Lewis and her sister are already on the Pimms. He drains the last of his bottle of beer. It went down well and has gone to his head. He feels as if he's on holiday himself.

He's just considering whether to have another one or not when there's an unexpected tremor that shakes the ceiling, a wailing from Eva and an almighty crash from upstairs. The only thing he can compare it to is the earth tremor that happened close by earlier in the year that had shaken the whole house. It had made you feel as if you were going to fall out of bed. 'Oh my God! Eva!'

Mr Lewis races upstairs. He tries to enter the bedroom, but something is blocking the door. He can hear moaning. 'Eva! What's going on? Let me in!'

'I can't. It's all gone wrong! I told you, Mr Lewis.'

Her voice has changed. It sounds much louder, more resonant.

'What do you mean, it's gone wrong? What's happened? Let me in! What's blocking the door?' He can hear her sobbing now. '*Eva!*' He tries shoving the door with his shoulder.

'Wait! You're hurting me!' she cries.

Something moves, an obstacle or weight, and the door suddenly gives, surprising him. He falls, stumbling, into the room, and then trips over something – a foot. A large foot; huge, in fact. Perfect, but huge. Mr Lewis gasps.

There, on the floor, her neck and shoulders hunched against the far wall, amongst the debris of the broken bed, is Eva. She's massive, four times the size of him, maybe, seemingly filling the room. She's naked, except for the white duvet she's clutching to her, just about covering her modesty. It's tucked between her legs, which are slightly parted, her knees up like gable ends. She looks distraught, and is weeping. 'I told you, Mr Lewis. I told you we shouldn't have done it!' Mr Lewis runs his hands through his hair.

'Make it go back. Have you tried to make it go back?'

'How? How can I do that?'

'I don't know. Reverse the combination or something? We discussed this, remember? What was it? You *can* remember the combination, can't you?' Eva looks at him, terrified. '*Can't you?*'

'I don't know! I can never remember them straightaway. I say so many, so quickly, once I get going, and I'm almost in a trance – once I've changed it goes straight out of my head. I know where I was, I think, but it'll take time. And then I'd have to reverse it, and I'd need to be calm so I can concentrate. it'll never work like this – if it works at all! You've got to stop pressuring me!' She breaks down again.

'I'm sorry. I'm sorry. Oh my God. What have we done? Look at the bed, look at the room. Look at you!' He studies her properly for the first time. This isn't a giantess –grotesque, clumsy and ugly – this is yards of lithe-limbed, bodacious perfection; think the '50s movie poster for *Attack of the 50 Foot Woman* – straddling that highway; that white wrap-around bikini top bursting with golden cleavage, that tiny matching skirt full of promise...

'*Shit! The curtains!*' Eva's large head and black hair are clearly visible through the window. Mr Lewis rushes over to close the curtains. The light in the room dims. 'But what went wrong?' he says, crouching down beside her, still trying to take her in – the sheer size of her. Her limbs go on forever. It makes him feel small, childlike.

'I don't know. I just wished I could grow big – like you said. Perhaps I should have been more specific and said human-sized.'

'Yes, I'd say you should.'

'Hold me, Mr Lewis. I'm scared.' Despite her size, Eva has never looked more vulnerable.

Mr Lewis moves towards her, but it's more a case of her holding him. She wraps her long arms around him, pressing his face to her hot, wet cheek, as if their physical roles have reversed. Her large tears dampen his face and hair. 'I'm a freak,' she sobs.

'No you're not, you're beautiful.'

'I am. I'm a freak. And what if I can't go back? What if I'm stuck like this? In this room, trapped?'

Mr Lewis is listening, but he's also aware that he's lying on the dome-shaped mound of one of her breasts. There's no ignoring it; its enormous. As she cries, it wobbles and jiggles; he can feel her nipple through the bed cover, rubbing and pressing against him. He feels a sudden, unexpected stirring in his loins that he cannot deny. This is his strongest emotion, overriding the fear and panic. His mind wanders at the possibilities…

CHAPTER 14

Out of desperation, Mr Lewis leaves the house and re-enters it to see if Eva will shrink back to her normal size. But she just turns into a giant, rigid, plastic doll, which is quite unnerving. He quickly wakes her again by touching her foot, not wanting to see her like that.

'See, I told you it wouldn't work. It's not like I lose my hearing or sight – or anything else I've unlocked – when I turn back,' Eva says.

'Well, it's got to be the numbers then, reversing them – it's the only way. Are you sure you've never tried it before?'

'Yes. Quite sure. Why would I want to go back to not being able to see or hear? I might not be able to unlock them again.'

Mr Lewis ponders this whilst feasting his eyes over the length of her again, unable to help himself. If she *could* turn back to normal, it might be forever. She may never be this size again; he'd never get her to agree to it – not after this trauma. There's something about this that gnaws at him. In this state he can do things with her, do things *to* her; this might be the only chance they get. He feels torn.

'OK, if we're going to do this I think we need to make you more comfortable. First, I'm going to get the room tidied up. Do you want a drink? Water or something?'

'Yes please. I *am* thirsty. It's so hot in here. Not too much, though, I don't want to, you know…' She trails off.

'Anything to eat? Are you hungry?'

'God, no!' Probably wise, he thinks.

'OK. I'll be back in a minute.'

Downstairs in the kitchen, Mr Lewis is trying to find something for Eva to drink out of. He spies an empty vase on the windowsill. Perfect. He gives it a good wash and rinse before half-filling it with cold water.

Eva accepts the water gratefully, clutching the vase in one hand like a beaker, whilst holding the duvet to her chest with her other hand. She drinks quickly and the water drips down her chin, her throat, her neck, down between those enticing, swollen mounds just visible above the cover. She passes the vase back to him. He takes it with both hands, placing it behind the curtain on the windowsill before setting about straightening the room.

The bed isn't in as bad a state as he first thought; possibly even salvageable. The main part that Eva is still lying on has merely dropped straight through, the bolts snapped clean off. These could probably be replaced or fixed back together with long screws. He feels a wave of relief at this as he props the footboard against the wall.

Eva: A grown-up fairy tale

He rights the upturned bedside tables and lamps, also placing them against the walls, trying to clear a space around Eva. She has so little room to manoeuvre. 'I feel so helpless,' she says miserably. 'I wish I could help you.'

'Don't worry, it's fine. I'm going to get you another mattress to lie on.'

'Can you get some more sheets too; this cover is too hot – and small.'

Mr Lewis fetches the single mattress from Lottie's room. He leaves it propped on the landing and pulls clean sheets out of the airing cupboard. His mind starts to tick again. Why is he in such a rush? They've got practically forty-eight hours for Eva to turn back, maybe more. And he feels confident that she'll be able to do this – why wouldn't she? He's talking himself into it. One night couldn't hurt, could it? He returns to the bedroom with the sheets.

Whilst he was gone, Eva has sat up more, her back against the window, her long, smooth legs stretched out in front of her, gazelle-like. There's not a blemish on them, not a vein, not a wrinkle. The duvet just comes to the top of her thighs, creating a dark v-shaped shadow between them, or at least he thinks it's a shadow. He feels overcome with lust. His hands are shaking as he passes her the sheets. He lingers awkwardly, expectantly.

'Well, go and get the mattress then – and wait out there a minute whilst I get decent,' she says. Mr Lewis is confused and disappointed; as brazen as she was when tiny, Eva now appears bashful about her nakedness in her new size – as if she's become ashamed of her body. He feels beseeching, desperate – a little boy – as he's ordered out of the room.

Out on the landing he's tormented by frustration. He can hear movement, rustling, Eva sighing as she moves about in the bedroom. It's like the first time she got undressed in the same room as him, but ten times worse. He imagines what she looks like naked, wants to put his eye to the crack in the doorway. He can feel himself hardening against the fly of his jeans, pressing against the material.

Stumbling into the bathroom, he splashes cold water on his face. He needs to calm down, to think of something else, but it's no use. Over the last few months a carnal hunger has been building – an appetite that needs sating. And that isn't a mere snack waiting in there; it's a banquet, a veritable feast. He looks at himself in the mirror and makes a decision.

Mr Lewis knocks on the door. 'Can I come in?'

'Wait a minute... yes.' He enters the room, clutching the mattress strategically in front of him. The room seems dark compared to the landing. Eva is wrapped in pale, lemon-coloured sheets, tucked under her arms and across her chest, like a dress. Her body's more covered now, which is a shame, but the comparative thinness of the material more than makes up for it. The sheets cling to her, forming shapes around her, leaving nothing to the imagination. And as for the colours – the pale yellow against her skin and jet-black hair – it takes his breath away. He wants to worship this goddess, this idol. Lifting her heavy feet and legs up, lovingly, one at a time, he slips the mattress underneath them and shunts it up against the other one. He then crawls towards her. 'Eva, I want you,' he says...

****

Afternoon turns into evening, evening turns into night, and Mr Lewis loses himself in the kingdom of her body; an intrepid explorer navigating unchartered terrain. Her breasts, a mountain range; between them a sticky, sweet-scented valley; the areolae of her nipples, perfectly pink and pleasantly pimpled. One thigh, a mile of golden sand – he rolls against it, writhes against it. Her raven hair, a whole world. Between her legs, a forest – a pagan place, musk-scented and warm. The vast, flat plain of her stomach, and in it the oasis of her belly button; a briny rockpool that he dips his tongue in and tastes.

He can't please a woman like this. But that doesn't stop him from pleasing himself. In fact, it turns him on more. The things she says: 'It just tickles, Mr Lewis,' 'You're too small,' 'You *are* funny, Mr Lewis.' Three times Peter disowned Jesus before the rooster crowed, and three times Mr Lewis betrays his wife, expelling himself against Eva, hardening again and again; the frustration and the fact that he can't satisfy her driving him on.

Eva endures it all resignedly, in a state of somewhat bemused detachment and shock. In the end she pleases herself, with long, slender fingers. Mr Lewis revels in the slick of honey this creates, whilst shushing her loud cries.

By early morning they are both spent. Eva has never been awake this long. She's shattered and far from comfortable. Mr Lewis rests his head on her chest in a dreamy languor. They try, but fail, to drift off – both of them too hot and uncomfortable. Opening a window isn't an option. In the end Mr Lewis gives up and goes to the spare room.

CHAPTER 15

He's pulled out of sleep by a strange sound, a rattling. His eyes are still closed but he can tell that it's morning. What time is it? Why is he aching? The sound seems to be coming from outside the front of the house. He hears a door opening and closing; he feels it: it reverberates through the house. *It's his front door! What the fuck?* His eyes shoot open – wide open in alarm. Why is he in the spare room? And who the hell's in his house? Suddenly, it all comes back to him. Last night. Eva. What has he done? *What has he fucking done?* He feels crippled by shame. To his horror, he hears the inner porch door into the lounge creak open.

Mr Lewis jumps up and rushes across the landing in his boxer shorts to Lottie's room, his heart pounding. He peers round the curtain, looking onto the front garden. They couldn't have come back early – why would they? There's an unfamiliar car across the driveway, blocking him in. A female voice from downstairs: 'Hello! Anybody home?' The voice sounds uncertain, frightened. It takes a few moments to register who it is ... Nicky, the cat lady. He forgot to call her! *Fuck!*

'Mr Lewis? Is that you?' He's got to say something, anything; otherwise she might come upstairs – or call the police!

'Hello! Yes, it's me. Be down in a minute!' he calls. Shit; his clothes – they're in his bedroom. He's going to have to cross the landing. 'Erm, sit yourself down! Won't be long!' He waits for a moment, then takes a deep breath and darts across the top of the stairs, hoping for the best. Nicky's leaning on the banister, looking up. Shit! She puts her head down in embarrassment when she sees him and retreats into the lounge.

Back in his marital bedroom, the seriousness of the situation hits home. The room's filled with a giant plastic doll. There are mattresses on the floor, sheets, a broken bed and upturned furniture. Mr Lewis rights a bedside cabinet and locates his jeans, having to manoeuvre one of Eva's legs as he does so. He quickly slips some clothes on and heads downstairs, closing the door firmly behind him.

'Nicky!' he says, descending the stairs in bare feet. 'I am *so* sorry. I was meant to call you.' Nicky looks uncomfortable with the situation; the fact that they barely know each other doesn't help. She appears to shrink back, rattling her keys defensively in front of her.

'Mr Lewis! You gave me a fright; I wasn't expecting you. I'm sure Dianne said Sunday.'

'No. Yes, she did. There was a change of plan, a deal that hasn't gone through – long story. Anyway, I'm not going till Monday evening now. I got left behind!' He laughs too loudly. 'And like I said, I was meant to call you and then I couldn't find your number, and then I clean forgot. It's entirely my fault.'

'Yes, I did wonder. I presumed you'd gone in one car, and then the front door wasn't locked. I didn't know what to think then. I thought maybe someone had got in the house.'

'No, no. Just me!' he laughs again. Just then, there's a thud from the bedroom upstairs. They both look up, then Nicky looks at Mr Lewis, her eyes narrowing slightly. 'That'll be the cat!' he says. 'Probably wants some breakfast.'

'Oh, do you want me to feed him while I'm here?'

'No, no. That's fine. It's a she actually. Stella.'

'Course it is. Silly me. I don't mind, really.'

'No, honestly. I'm sorry you've had a wasted journey that's all.'

'Oh, it's no bother. I'd have been coming over anyway.'

There's an awkward pause. Why won't she just piss off? I hope she's not expecting a coffee or something, thinks Mr Lewis. He yawns and stretches.

'Right, I'd better be getting...' Nicky is interrupted by another noise – this time a bang at the back door; the cat flap. Poor Stella; she'd been locked out all night. They both look at each other again. Then the cat appears at the patio door, miaowing to be let in. Mr Lewis shifts uncomfortably and clears his throat.

'Must have got out of a window.' He goes to let her in. 'Hello, girl!' he says, bending down to pet her. 'Are you hungry?' All the while, he's praying there will be no more noises from upstairs. What the hell was that

Eva: A grown-up fairy tale

anyway? Nicky finally gets the hint and makes to leave. 'Sorry again for the confusion, and it'll be Tuesday now. I'm still here tomorrow,' he reminds her as she goes. He closes the door and watches from behind the lounge curtain as she gets in her car. As she drives off, she looks up at the bedroom windows. They are all closed.

Mr Lewis stands there for a while, head in hands, before returning upstairs; the enormity of what's just happened, the reality of what lies ahead and all these close shaves overwhelming him. Shame washes over him again in waves when he thinks back to the previous night; he feels dirty, debased – a deviant. He wants to cry. He misses his family and wants everything to go back to normal; wants *her* to go back to normal.

Wearily, he trudges up the stairs. It's as if he can't face Eva, doesn't want to deal with her awake. He doesn't want to see her as she is – a giant doll – either. If only these changes had a time limit – twenty-four hours, say – then they wouldn't be in this mess. But they haven't; they are forever. And she's no longer something you can hide; he can't just walk out of the house, turn her back into a doll and stick her in a box. *What has he done?*

Eva has slipped down the wall because he moved her leg – that was what the bump must have been. He hesitates for a moment, preparing himself before waking her up. She melts back to life. 'Who was it, Mr Lewis?' Her voice seems too loud.

'The lady who feeds the cat – I forgot to cancel her. I think she knew something was going on; she saw me run across the landing. She heard a noise too.' He forces himself to look Eva in the face. She looks tired – human-tired; dark circles under her eyes. 'Eva, you've got to change back. Right away. I've got to get this bed fixed, the room straightened up. I can't do it with you in here.'

'Don't you think I know that, Mr Lewis? It's not that easy. Do you think I want to be like this?' She looks as if she's about to cry again. 'I feel dirty. I want a bath.'

'Well, you just need to get on with it now, so start concentrating.'

'Oh, you've changed your tune. You weren't in any rush yesterday!'

'That was yesterday. We're running out of time. You need to remember the combination and reverse it – it's the only way. Then you can have a bath.'

'Come here first, Mr Lewis. It's going to take a while.' She holds out her arms. He reluctantly lets her hug him. It just feels wrong this morning, her being so big; there's nothing erotic or lustful about it.

'Do you regret it?' she says.

'What?'

'Last night... I don't.'

'No,' he says quickly, but can't look her in the eye as he disengages himself from her suffocating embrace. He turns away.

'Mr Lewis.'

'Yes.'

'Before I start, I'm afraid I need to go.'

'Go where?'

'You know ... *go*; I need a pee.'

'Oh God.' He pulls a face. This is getting tedious, gross even. 'I'll get a bucket,' he says wearily.

'I think some sort of tray might be better.'

After returning with a deep-sided oven tray, Mr Lewis leaves her to it. He doesn't want to see any more; he's had enough.

CHAPTER 16

It's a Sunday, normally a day of relaxation: warm croissants from the garage and a perusal of the newspaper (sports section first) before a full English breakfast. This morning Mr Lewis feels neither relaxed nor hungry; his stomach is in knots. Lottie would usually go with him to get the croissants and paper; this prompts him to wonder what they're doing. His phone! Where is it? He can't remember seeing it since the previous afternoon. Dianne was bound to have texted him to say goodnight.

His mobile is on the coffee table in the lounge, where he left it. To his alarm, he has two texts and a missed call, all from Dianne. He vaguely remembers the house phone ringing the previous evening as well. He ignored it; he'd been in the throes of lust. What had he been thinking? What would Dianne be thinking? He's got some explaining to do.

He'll ring her on the way to the garage; he needs some fresh air, away from the confines of the house.

He's getting cabin fever, and as Eva said it could take a while. Why shouldn't he do his own thing? Try and be normal? But he can't leave the house – she'll turn to plastic again. But isn't that a good thing? Didn't she say she could concentrate better when she was asleep? Sod it, he'll go. Should he tell her or just leave? Just leave – don't get involved and leave her to it; it'll only distract her.

Hearing his wife's and his daughter's voices is good. But it brings back those feelings of guilt and hammers home the despicable things he's been doing. They both sound so innocent, so trusting. He tells them he'd gone out with Ian, making the most of the free weekend. They went to play pool at the pub in Ian's village – where there's no reception. One thing led to another and they ended up in town for a few and got horribly drunk – Chinese takeaway, the lot. No, not 'town' town (Dianne associated Ian with lap-dancing clubs and cocaine), just the market square. He has a hangover this morning. 'Ditto,' says Mrs Lewis. Mr Lewis says goodbye and hangs up, thinking he's going to hell for all these lies.

Walking down his street as he returns home gives him a strange feeling. All the houses are relatively the same: the same garage doors, the same front lawns, the same front porches, the same upstairs windows. If only anyone knew what's upstairs in *his* house right now. What secrets lie behind these other facades of suburban normality – in garages and spare rooms, attics, lofts and pantries? Or is it just him?

Back inside, he considers checking on Eva's progress but decides against it. It's too soon. He makes a coffee, eats his croissants and, with the cat for company, reads the paper, but struggles to concentrate. There certainly won't be a cooked breakfast today, not that he fancies one; the fridge is pretty much bare.

Impatience and curiosity soon get the better of him. What if Eva's already turned back to her normal size? She didn't have to be awake to get sight or hearing. What if she's lying on the floor right now, waiting for him? If only this is true. He could be wasting precious time – he could be getting the bed fixed.

Mr Lewis heads upstairs. He quietly pushes open the bedroom door, crossing his fingers. Peering round it, to his dismay, he finds nothing has changed. Eva is still the same size. This causes his heart to jolt in panic again, and he mutters and curses before leaving the room, not wanting to distract her any more than necessary.

He takes a much-needed shower. His mind keeps tormenting him. What if they run out of time? What if she can't turn back at all? What then? This doesn't bear thinking about. His life would be over: his marriage, his career. He's not willing to let this happen. Desperate times call for desperate measures. When pushed, when backed into a corner, men can be capable of anything. You see it time and time again. An affair turned sour, the threat of being outed to the wife and family, women being bumped off. If it came to it – really came to it – he'd have to get rid of Eva. But how? Hack her up into plastic logs whilst she was still a doll? It was like something from that horror movie *Asylum*. She'd probably come back to life and haunt him.

Jesus, what was he thinking? It won't come to that. It *can't* come to that. Don't think about it. Try not to panic. It's not going to help. His rational self kicks in

– the strategist in him. He needs to form a plan, stay focused. First, he needs to get the room straightened up; check out the damage to the bed properly; see if he needs to get some parts for it – or even a new bed. Feeling better, with a goal to work towards, he steps out of the shower.

Returning to his room for underwear, a towel wrapped round his waist, Mr Lewis wakes Eva up to check on her progress. She's in the way anyhow; he can't get to his bedside drawer with her lying the way she is, rigid. He touches her leg and there's a discernible hum under his hand, not a vibration, not as strong as that, but something at least; this is good news. It fades away as she comes round. This takes longer than usual – as if she was in a deep trance, or maybe she's just getting more tired; it certainly appears that way.

'Mr Lewis,' she says, her voice slurry, 'You startled me.' She shifts position, and as she does so her sheets slip off, revealing her nakedness. Mr Lewis feels a fleeting stirring of lust – his body's knee-jerk reaction to a flashback from last night – but then it's gone again. She covers herself. 'Why are you in a towel?' She looks surprised.

'I had a shower. I need to get some boxers.'

'All right for some,' she says.

'How's it going? I felt something when I touched your leg.' He turns his bedside table round and pulls out some underwear.

'Good and bad. I think I've remembered the combination from last night, but reversing it doesn't seem to be working – so far anyway; unless it's not the right one. So I'm trying something else and I'm starting to get somewhere. I can feel it.'

'Good,' he says, relieved.

To his surprise, Eva reaches out a large hand and curls it round his torso and back. It feels sensitive to the touch – the last thing he needs, standing in a towel. He feels an involuntary twitch down below. 'Come and lie with me, Mr Lewis. Just for a while. I miss you and I hate being like this. I want us to spend time together, whilst we've still got the chance.'

'No, Eva, not like this,' he says, removing her hand. 'We haven't got time. You need to be your proper size. Then we can.'

Eva looks hurt. 'But I'll be tiny again. And what then? What good is that to us?'

'It means we can go back to normal, that's what. And at least we'll know it can be done. There will be other times. But if we don't get you back and get this bed fixed up, there won't be other times – ever; it'll all be over. Can't you see that?' He turns to leave the room, clutching his boxer shorts, exasperated and running out of patience.

'Where are you going?' she asks.

'To get changed.'

'Well, why do you have to leave the room?' Mr Lewis gives her a look, too proud to admit that he feels embarrassed at the size difference between them in the cold light of day. He closes the door.

'I wish I was your size!' Eva calls. The door rattles in its frame as she bangs a fist on the floor in frustration.

CHAPTER 17

After dressing, Mr Lewis returns to the room to inspect the bed properly, telling Eva to ignore him and to keep on concentrating. He needs some wood glue and some new bolts – the type with holes in them. And if possible a few new slats too. He remembers the shop he got the bed from. It was on the retail park, which means it'll be open today.

Once again, he leaves the house, leaving Eva to it – glad to have something to focus on. He stops at a cash machine; it wouldn't do to have DIY and bed shop purchases on their joint bank statement. He commends himself on still thinking clearly. All the bits he requires are in stock, except for the slats. 'Would you like me to order some for you, sir?' the shop assistant asks.

'No thanks, I'll manage.' He'll have to.

Mr Lewis chucks his purchases on the passenger seat. He's about to start the engine when he realises how hungry he is – starving, in fact. He seems to have

Eva: A grown-up fairy tale

got his appetite back. No wonder, really; he hasn't eaten a proper meal since Saturday lunchtime. There's a plethora of fast food outlets on the retail park. His stomach rumbles. He's not really a fan of junk food, but today it could be just the thing. He feels as if he actually *is* hungover, and craves something salty. He'd have to buy something to cook at home anyway, and he can't be bothered with that.

Sitting there, tucking into a burger, Mr Lewis is surrounded by families, children, fathers; some of whom look back at him. He feels like a bachelor, a single man – lonely beyond belief; a snapshot of the future, maybe? He misses his family terribly, and almost chokes as an unexpected sob rises in his throat. Not for the first time, he feels as if he will break down, right here in front of everyone. He drains the rest of his milk, packs the half-eaten meal onto a tray and leaves, still hungry.

No longer thinking clearly, Mr Lewis drives round the roundabout more times than he has to, feeling lost and a little unhinged. He takes the long way home; anything to pass the time.

Back home, he goes straight upstairs. He can't help himself. Surely there must have been a breakthrough by now? The day's slipping away. But Eva is still the same. He puts his hand on her leg, momentarily forgetting that this is going to wake her up. The vibrations are stronger, much stronger; they reverberate through his hand and up his arm. They fade away again as she wakes up.

She comes to, even more slowly than before. She's grouchy. 'Mr Lewis, you've got to stop waking me up! Do you want me to change or not? I was really getting somewhere then!'

'I'm sorry,' he says, feeling like a naughty little boy who's been scolded. 'I just wanted to check the vibrations. Do you want me to go outside again, so you can concentrate?'

'No. Don't. I'm getting close to something. I want to be awake when it happens. Ow! My head aches,' she says. 'Can you pass me my water?'

As he watches her drink, it strikes him again how exhausted she looks; as if all this effort has taken an immense toll on her. If she looked tired before, she now looks like a woman who's been in labour for hours on end; her hair is lank, there are bags under her eyes and her skin is pale and clammy. It's a shame to see this considering how perfect she was before. She passes the vase back. He touches her arm briefly, then slips out of the room before she asks for anything else.

As he tries for a second time to read the newspaper, lying on the sofa, Mr Lewis keeps nodding off, overcome with tiredness; a combination of the lack of sleep and all the stress. Soon he stops battling it. The paper drops to the floor and he snuggles into a cushion. He begins to snore...

****

When Mr Lewis wakes, to his amazement the light outside is beginning to fade. Jesus, how long has he been asleep? He reaches for his phone. It's gone half past eight. He must have slept for seven or eight hours solid. How is that possible? There are a couple of missed texts on his phone again. Damn it! Why did that keep happening? He's running out of excuses.

Mr Lewis is just about to check the texts when he

Eva: A grown-up fairy tale

becomes aware of sounds from the kitchen – a cupboard door opening, then closing. What the hell? He groggily rises from the sofa, still half-asleep. Did he imagine it? Next he hears a tap being turned on, this time all too clearly. Is Dianne back? Has Nicky returned? Has Eva finally shrunk, and then somehow managed to get up on the counter? He shuffles through the empty lounge and slowly pushes open the kitchen door, fearing the worst.

There, with her back to him, drinking a glass of water, is his wife. Or at least he thinks it's his wife. He rubs his eyes. She's wearing Dianne's clothes: a blouse, jeans and white pumps. She's about the same size as his wife. But her hair is different – darker, longer. He gasps. She turns around to face him, aware of his presence...

Mr Lewis puts his fist to his mouth in shock. It's Eva. About five foot five. But she looks terrible – a shadow of her former self, as if all the life has been sucked from her. 'I've done it, Mr Lewis; exactly what you wanted. We can be together now, compatible at last, forever.'

'No,' he cries. 'That's not what I wanted at all!'

'But you *did* want it, didn't you, before I grew big? You wanted me to be human-sized, wife-sized – so you could *do* me. Well, you can now.' She begins to unbutton the blouse, which is a little too big for her. 'How do you want it, Mr Lewis? On all fours, like you and Mrs Lewis in Cornwall?'

'No!' he cries again. '*Stop!* I've got a wife. I don't need another one. I want you to be small again!'

'It's too late for that now. I'm not turning back ... ever. You can't make me. You're not putting me back in a box again. I'm pulling the strings now. You can be *my* plaything.' She's reached the bottom button of her blouse – his wife's blouse – and it falls open. Something is wrong here too. Her stomach is too thin, sunken, her skin sallow, her ribs showing, her breasts – what there is of them – two small sacks that have lost their stuffing. She begins to laugh and reaches for the button of her jeans.

Mr Lewis sees a threat – a hideous threat to him and his family; nothing else; something that needs snuffing out once and for all. He rushes to the utensil drawer, the third one down, the one where they keep the heavy wooden rolling pin, and pulls it out. She sees his intention and flies at him, grabbing his arm with both hands and dragging it down as they struggle.

****

'Mr Lewis!'

'No!' he cries.

'Mr Lewis! Wake up!'

Mr Lewis comes round. He's still on the sofa. It's still light. Something is pulling on his arm. There's a little voice. He opens his eyes. Eva is staring up at him, her face a picture of fright and concern. She's beautiful again – looking tired, but tiny and blessed and beautiful. 'Mr Lewis, you were dreaming. I couldn't wake you. I've been calling you for ages, but you didn't hear me. I had to open the door by myself and come down. I was worried the cat might be down here.'

'You've done it!' he says. 'You've actually done it! Oh, you wonderful thing!' He scoops her up and pops her onto his chest, holding her too tight.

'Careful, Mr Lewis! You're hurting me.'

'I'm sorry. I'm just so pleased to see you back.'

'Well, it *was* what you wanted, wasn't it?' Mr Lewis doesn't say anything, still disturbed by the dream. 'It was, wasn't it?'

'Yes, it was.'

'Cause I personally wouldn't have minded...'

'Don't say it!' he says, stopping her. 'I think we've had enough excitement for now. We need to get that bed fixed.' Even that, in comparison, after the dream he's had, seems a mere trifle – something that can be explained away or replaced – such is the euphoria he feels. 'Come on, let's go upstairs.'

'Can I get something to eat first, Mr Lewis? I'm starving!' This makes him smile.

CHAPTER 18

The bed is fixed as well as can be – bolts replaced and cracks repaired, slats glued back together – and the bedroom is put back to normal. That evening, whilst Eva is having her much-longed-for bath, Mr Lewis makes a point of calling his wife and Lottie, to tell them both he's missing them and can't wait to see them. 'Fingers crossed for tomorrow,' Mrs Lewis says. 'Hope it all goes through all right.' What with all the weekend's commotion, Mr Lewis isn't sure what she's talking about at first; the delayed completion day has completely slipped his mind.

He and Eva spend one last night together; more out of necessity than anything – the glue needs to set on the bed, so they sleep in the spare room instead.

They both sleep well, and by morning Eva has a bit of colour back in her cheeks and her hair has regained its shine. Mr Lewis expects to have butterflies in his stomach and a buzz of anticipation about the deal going through, but strangely he feels nothing.

Eva: A grown-up fairy tale

Despite it being a Monday, he decides to sit it out in his office; perhaps it will help him to get into a professional frame of mind. Eva's a little put out, considering these are their last remaining hours together for a while. She wants to watch him leave out of the bedroom window, but he refuses, saying someone might see her.

Mr Lewis walks to work, thinking it will clear his head, blow out the cobwebs, before reaching the office. It's a big day after all. But his mind keeps turning over the rollercoaster of the weekend's events, the ups and downs; weighing up the eroticism he felt against the horror it eventually became; the panic when he thought Eva would stay big forever, culminating in that horrific dream. He'd thought it was real – he really had. How trapped he'd felt; at her mercy – the hatred and violence he'd felt towards her. Was that a vision of the future?

Mr Lewis stops dead in his tracks. Fortunately he hasn't reached the main road yet, otherwise it would look a bit odd. He's behind some houses, on a cut-through screened by trees. He comes to a decision. Instead of carrying on, he turns around and heads back home. On the way, he makes a phone call.

Mr Lewis lets himself back into the house. He puts down his briefcase and goes upstairs to Lottie's room. Eva isn't in the box where he left her. She's on her back at the bottom of a curtain; she'd tried to climb up to see out of the window after all.

He picks her up. She feels so good in his hand, so small. It's a wonderful feeling to have his power back, to have regained control. She wriggles to life, just like the old days. 'Mr Lewis! This is a surprise. Couldn't you keep away from me?'

'Yes, something like that. Eva, listen to me. I've got another surprise for you – an even bigger one this time. I've been thinking. I want us to go away – me and you, forever. Somewhere where nobody knows us.' Eva's big brown eyes grow wider still. She squeals in excitement.

'Are you serious? Just me and you?'

'Yes.'

'But where?'

'I haven't decided yet. Somewhere by the seaside, maybe. We'll just get in the car and drive.'

'But what made you decide?'

'This weekend, I suppose. And then going back to work – *you* going back to normal. Thinking about what you've achieved. Knowing that you can change your size when you want – the possibilities are endless! We just need the time and the space. Imagine it, you could finally unlock going outside!'

'So when? Now? Are we going now? Put me down, Mr Lewis, I need to get packed!' She starts to wriggle.

'Wait. Hold your horses. We can't go yet. You need to listen to me carefully. We can get packed but we can't go till later. This deal is going through, remember. It's really important – for us as well now. When it has, then we can go. And we'll be in a hurry; that's why we need to get packed now.'

'But what about Mrs Lewis and Lottie? I feel kind of sorry for them.'

'Let me deal with that. I'll tell them when we get there. Lottie will understand – she's still young; she can come and visit us. Right, grab what you want to take with you and I'll go and get a suitcase.' He puts her down.

Eva: A grown-up fairy tale

Mr Lewis rushes to the bedroom to grab the little black suitcase from the top of the wardrobe. It isn't there. They've taken it with them. 'Shit!' It'll have to be a holdall. He rushes downstairs to grab a holdall and brings it back. Eva's rummaging around in the toy box, chucking things out. Mr Lewis grabs some underwear, a towel, his toothbrush, deodorant, a change of clothes, and returns to stick them in the bag. 'Have you got everything you need?'

'I think so.' She's got clothes, a hairbrush, her toilet pan. Mr Lewis shoves them all in the bag. 'You're not taking much.'

'We haven't got room. Besides, most of my stuff is already in Norfolk at the caravan. Now, I need you to get in and make yourself comfortable.'

'Why do I need to get in now?'

'Because, like I said, we're going to be in a rush later. I just need to grab the bag, get in the car and go. You'll go to sleep the second I leave the house anyway, so what does it matter?'

'I know, but I'll be stuck in a bag for hours.'

'Well, I'll leave it half-unzipped. The minute we're in the car I'll get you out.' Eva pouts.

'Come on,' he says, and picks her up. Reluctantly, she lies down in the bag. He puts her on a towel to make her comfortable.

Mr Lewis lingers, taking her in, looking serious. Eva notices. 'What's wrong, Mr Lewis?'

'Nothing. Just that you're so beautiful, that's all. And I'm going to miss you.'

'Well, it's only a few hours... Mr Lewis?'

'Yes, Eva.'

'Can I make myself human-sized next time?'

'Yes, course you can. Next time.' He strokes her raven hair with his thumb and then brushes it across her face. She kisses it.

'Bye, Eva.' He half-zips up the bag.

'Bye, Mr Lewis. See you on the other side.'

* * * * * * * *

After a tense morning at the office, the money goes through just before lunch. Keys are handed over and there are sighs of relief all round. Mr Lewis calls his wife to tell her the good news.

* * * * * * * *

Ian slips down the alleyway and round the back of the Lewises' house. He retrieves the patio door key from its hiding place. Letting himself in, he doesn't know whether to be amused or concerned at this unexpected request from his old buddy – especially all the cloak and dagger stuff. He hopes he's not in trouble. But Stephen isn't the type to get mixed up in trouble – he's as straight as they come; trouble is *his* department. He'd sounded OK. Just pick up the suitcase – no, holdall, he'd texted him about that little change of plan – and get rid of it. God knows why. It seems strange that the bag is in his kid's bedroom. But there it is; a blue holdall with yellow straps, just as described.

The one thing Stephen *had* been adamant about was not to look in it. Just take it somewhere, anywhere. And don't tell him where; he didn't want to know any details about it. What has he got in it? Has the cat died or something? A gimp suit, maybe? A dark secret?

Dirty money? The bag doesn't feel too heavy. It's half-unzipped, making it tempting to have a quick peek. No, better not. Don't get involved.

The cat's downstairs. Ian gives it a stroke, then lets himself out of the patio door, replacing the key.

He begins to sweat, and looks around before getting back in his car. It feels as if he's in a movie as he puts the bag on the passenger seat. He knows exactly where he's going to take it: the perfect spot – a place known locally as The Eyrie, the highest spot overlooking Rutland Water. In the back of his car are a couple of bricks. He'd considered the recycling site, but it would look too suspicious; besides, they've got CCTV there.

Ian negotiates a roundabout, then drives through a few villages. All the while, he keeps looking across at the holdall. What the hell's in there? He puts some music on to try and forget about it, but it's no use. Before long, he's on the main road towards Rutland Water. The reservoir sparkles in the sun, and the road steepens. Again, he looks across at the holdall. Surely one little peek couldn't hurt.

Keeping one eye on the road and one hand on the wheel, he reaches over and slowly unzips the bag. He slips his hand inside and rummages around, hoping he doesn't get bitten or come up against the feel of rubber. 'Come on, you dirty old bugger. What have you got in here? Let Uncle Ian have a little look.' His hand immediately settles on something. Something he isn't expecting. Running his hand up and down it, he feels hair and legs and arms. It feels like a doll. 'What the hell?' he says. What's so dangerous about a doll? Perhaps it's one of Lottie's toys that they want to get rid of without her knowing. Seems a bit extreme, though.

He picks the doll up and props it on the seat next to the holdall, thinking there has to be something else in there. Still, she's a pretty thing; his eyes keep getting drawn back to her. He begins to rummage again, whilst at the same time trying to drive in a straight line. Just then, out of the corner of his eye, the doll starts to move of its own accord. Surely he's imagining it. Perhaps he's pressed a switch on it by mistake. It's rubbing its eyes and shaking its wrists out in front of it. Ian can't take his eyes off it. It turns its head slowly towards him and smiles. It has beautiful white teeth with a gap in them. 'What the fuck!' he says.

'Oh, thank you, Uncle Ian, thank you!' it says in return. 'I knew you wouldn't let me down! I've been waiting for so long. I just needed to be touched by a man...'

The doll doesn't get chance to finish. It's interrupted by the sudden blast of a car horn. Ian turns back to the road in shock. He's on the wrong side, careering headfirst into the path of an oncoming car. He swerves sharply but overcompensates, sending his own car into a slide. He tries to brake and turn the wheel, but it's too late. The heavy old Saab smashes straight through the wooden fence on the approach to The Eyrie. After going into a short freefall, the car lands violently on a rocky outcrop, smashing the windscreen and windows out. It does a full somersault before splashing right way up into the reservoir. With a hiss of steam and a belch of bubbles, it's sucked slowly under.

Moments later, the couple from the other car appear at the top of the hill. There's no sign of the Saab or of its driver; just some residual ripples on the surface of the water. As the man scrambles for his phone, his wife nudges him and points. '*Look!*' Various bits of debris have begun to float up to the surface of the water – a blue holdall with yellow straps, its contents spilled out; deodorant, a toothbrush, a man's underwear. It's hard to make out clearly, but there appear to be miniature clothes too – jackets, dresses... The couple, already shaken up, look at each other in wonder.

With trembling hands, the man dials the police. 'Hello! I'd like to report an accident at Rutland Water. We need urgent assistance!'

'What service do you require?' says the operator. The man falters, not hearing. 'Hello? Sir? Can you hear me?'

Before their eyes, a little doll has popped up onto the surface of the water – a little doll in a satiny blue dress with red lips and jet-black hair.

ABOUT THE AUTHOR

Adam Longden was born in Derby, England. He moved way out in the sticks to the edge of Nottinghamshire at the age of four, and has lived in the East Midlands ever since.

His debut novel, The Caterpillar Girl, was published in October 2016, followed by the sequel, Seaside Skeletons, in July 2019.

Eva: A Grown-up Fairy Tale is his first novella.

CONTACT THE AUTHOR

www.adamlongden.com

www.facebook.com/adamlongdenauthor

MORE BOOKS BY ADAM LONGDEN

The Caterpillar Girl

Seaside Skeletons

Printed in Great Britain
by Amazon